NUNATAK\FICTION

Nunatak is an Inuktitut word meaning "lonely peak," a rock or mountain rising above ice. During Quaternary glaciation in North America these peaks stood above the ice sheet and so became refuges for plant and animal life. Magnificent nunataks, their bases scoured by glaciers, can be seen along the Highwood Pass in the Alberta Rocky Mountains and on Ellesmere Island.

Nunataks are especially selected works of outstanding fiction by new western writers. The editors of Nunataks for NeWest Press are Aritha van Herk and Rudy Wiebe.

MOON Honey

Suzette Mayr

NeWest

Canadian Cataloguing in Publication Data

Mayr, Suzette.
  Moon honey

(Nunatak new fiction)
    ISBN 1-896300-00-6
    I Title. II. Series.
PS8576. A9M6 1995 C813′ .54 C95-910732-0
PR9199.3.M39M6 1995

Editor for the Press: Aritha van Herk
Editorial Coordinator: Eva Radford
Cover design: Evita McConnell Graphics
Book design: Chao Yu

NeWest Press gratefully acknowledges the financial assistance of The
Canada Council; The Alberta Foundation for the Arts, a beneficiary of
the Lottery Fund of the Government of Alberta; and The NeWest
Institute for Western Canadian Studies.

Printed and bound in Canada

NeWest Publishers Limited
Suite 310, 10359 - 82 Avenue
Edmonton, Alberta T6E 1Z9

COMMITTED TO THE DEVELOPMENT OF CULTURE AND THE ARTS

ACKNOWLEDGEMENTS

Huge, huge, no word can describe how huge the thanks owed to Aritha van Herk, Nicole Markotic, and Lisa Brawn for their suggestions and editorial advice. Thanks especially to Nicole for that last minute, beyond the call of duty midnight stint.

I would also like to thank my lovely parents, Rose-Marie and Ulrich Mayr, for their professional advice in the areas of nursing and geology respectively, as well as for their unlimited love and support. Thank you to Julien and Friedrich W. Mayr for their love and encouragement.

Thanks is also due to Kari Brawn and Gary McMillan, Kelly and Chris Venour, and Deb Dudek and Oz Filippin for inviting me to their weddings.

I want to acknowledge the instructors and students in the creative writing programs at the University of Calgary and the University of Alberta for providing me with the training and community necessary for the completion of this book.

For Lisa Brawn

My purpose is to tell of bodies which have been transformed into shapes of a different kind.

Metamorphoses
Ovid

Store the gown in a cedar chest or a lined wooden drawer. Air it out yearly and fold it in different places before restoring. Make sure it is stored in a dark, dry place.

Planning a Wedding to Remember:
The Perfect Wedding Planner
Beverly Clark

Carmen and Griffin begin dating the day she turns eighteen, back when she is still a white girl. When she is eighteen and a half they make love for the third time under the pool table in his parents' basement, she knocks her head on the table leg, and her skull roars with pain while Griffin pumps, his eyes closed. Her eyes roll back until the whites gleam pearl, her bottom jaw drops, and when she comes to she figures she's been unconscious for about a minute. Griffin takes about fifty-eight seconds. Carmen's timed him. They've timed each other. Griffin fifty-eight seconds, Carmen ten minutes — they've learned that orgasm speed relies on biology, the difference between men and women. Some of her girlfriends never have orgasms. Griffin's buddies, on the other hand, have no problem. Men and women.

They have concussive sex in the same room as the wooden inlay picture of three happy black people,

1

Africans she supposes, with long thin necks, baskets on their heads, thick red lips and gold hoops in their ears. Under the pool table they can lie relaxed and sweaty, side by side, and look up at the picture, the only decoration on any of the walls. A souvenir, Griffin says, a souvenir his mother picked up on one of her business trips.

Where? asks Carmen.

I don't know, some place where blacks live, obviously.

His mother, Fran, doesn't like Carmen at all. Carmen is not the kind of girl Fran would choose for her son, not the kind of girl Fran wants included in her family's bloodline. Carmen doesn't talk, slides in and out of Fran's house without so much as hello or goodbye, as though Fran were invisible or merely a servant. Fran only ever knows if Carmen is somewhere in the house from her grimy sneakers parked in the front hall, or the normally immaculate ashtrays crammed with lipsticked cigarette butts. Griffin and Carmen disappear for hours, the entire day sometimes, slam the front door or the back door or the patio door when they're back from wherever they go. Six P.M., a door slams and Griffin asks, when's supper Mom? just like nothing's happened, and the next thing Fran knows, Griffin is stuffing an entire bowl of green salad into his mouth and Carmen's beside him at the dinner table holding out her plate as if Fran owes her food. Fran's mother would have slapped that plate out of Carmen's hand, then slapped Carmen hard in the face. The least

Carmen can do is help clear up. Fran is tired of being her servant.

Have some more green salad, Carmen, Fran says, and whips the bowl of salad across the table.

Fran also disapproves of the premarital sex she knows Carmen and her son are having. Fran isn't stupid, she wasn't born yesterday. Sex is for people mature enough, financially stable enough, to handle an accident. She wouldn't put it past Carmen to get pregnant just to get her bitten nails into Griffin now, while he's still young, with so much promise. Oh yes, Fran's laid down the rules, no Carmen in the bedroom, no closed doors in the house, all the lights on the moment the sun goes down. She doesn't approve of the two of them disappearing for entire days, or Griffin arriving home at four o'clock in the morning, but she refrains from commenting because even if Fran doesn't like Carmen, at least Griffin isn't homosexual. At least he's sticking to girls, whorish and unmannered as Carmen may be.

Now if he was out until four o'clock in the morning with some strange boy, she'd certainly have something to say. Ida Sorensen down the street found out her son was homosexual, walked in on him and some young fella kissing for God's sake. God knows what would've happened if poor Ida'd walked in just ten minutes later. God knows. Fran would kill herself first. Carmen is a quiet and devious little tart, but maybe Carmen can learn. Be changed. Converted.

When Carmen turns twenty, Fran hints during Sunday dinner that they should be thinking about marriage. She wants to see grandchildren before she dies. St. Francis, she says, is a beautiful church. Carmen doesn't say anything — she doesn't believe in God or St. Francis or church or marriage — and Griffin chomps with his lips drawn back on the tail of his steak. He's a vegetarian when he's not in his mother's house; he doesn't become a meat-eater until he goes home at night. Fran sulks if he doesn't eat her dinners.

We were thinking maybe we'd just live together eventually, Ma. He chews the steak slowly, doesn't eat the fat, doesn't suck at the juice, doesn't let the bloody flesh touch his lips.

Oh, well, if that's what you want, says Fran, stacks the dishes loudly, one on top of the other so that long chords of steak fat lop down over the rims. If that's what you want, but her face says, Closed for Business. If her body were a section of land, she would be surrounded by coils of barbed wire, protected by Doberman pinschers snarling No Trespassing. No Ingrate Sons Allowed.

Fran married Godfrey when she was seventeen — too young, she should have waited until she was at least twenty. Twenty is a good age for marriage, old enough for babies, but still young enough to adapt to a husband's habits. Twenty. The ideal age. At the age of seventeen, Fran took Godfrey's name and he took her hand and

4

everything else. God could be a good husband for the right woman. If she believed in him. But God does what he wants, leaves every summer to do "research" (Fran still doesn't know what he does exactly), comes home hairy and smelly and unwashed and leaking other women's bodies and juices. God pretends to listen to her; he nods at the ends of her sentences, follows her with his eyes when she stands up and gestures with her hands to clarify a certain important point about her life, and makes sympathetic grunts when she complains about Griffin's late nights, but she can see God's watching a television set with a much more interesting show in his head. Why should she believe in her husband? Stand by her man? How can she believe in someone who doesn't pay attention to a single word she utters, just nods like a rocking horse, and empties his pipes into her scrubbed ashtrays, praises her cooking even when she microwaves TV dinners, and is always always on top?

Most of the time God doesn't listen to Fran because he doesn't know what to make of her. What does she want from him? Does she think his line of work involves psychiatry? He has yet to figure out what to say in response to her ravings. All he wants to do is prepare for his next field trip, make sure things go off without a hitch, smoke his pipe at the end of a good day's work.

He thinks of Fran sometimes when he's in the field, as he clomps from one fist-sized rock to the next, trying to keep his balance; he thinks about when they first married, their relationship now grey on grey on grey like the landscape he works in. Part of his work is following musk oxen, gathering samples of their stools. He crouches on the ground. He never promised her a rose garden, he never promised he'd be a stay-at-home husband and she seemed satisfied with their arrangement last time he talked to her. How many years ago was that? He can't even remember how long they've been married. Maybe he should wire her some flowers. What kind of flowers? One of those ready-made bouquets. They have nothing in common any more, and it's mostly her fault, although he's prepared to take some of the blame. She thinks his work is irrelevant, doesn't even know what he does.

He crouches in the gravel and the fabric of his weatherproof pants gathers behind his knees and in his crotch. Maybe he should have given her more children, maybe that would have kept her busy longer. He scoops a chilled bit of dung into his bare hands and rolls the sample around, rolls it between his fingers, brings it up to his nose now and then, lets it grow warmer and warmer in his palms until it reflects the heat of his hands. He pulls whiskers from his beard and adds them to the heated sample, rolls some more until the sample starts to simmer, then boil in his hands. The sample buzzes, starts to vibrate angrily. He breathes into his hands, opens his palms skyward. For Chrissakes Fran, he feels like saying, I'm only human.

A cloud of newly-made mosquitoes swells from his fingers. In new-born disorientation the mosquitoes burst from his hands like water from a fountain and fly up into the sky. Godfrey checks his hands to make sure they've all flown away, claps away any remaining dried stool, wipes his hands on his pants, then wipes the sweat off his forehead. Brand new mosquitoes. A fine crop, they looked like. He loves this job.

When Carmen and Griffin are together they are so much in love. These are the kind of dishes we'll buy, says Carmen. Brown ceramic. That's my favourite. Earthy. I just can't do porcelain.

Mine too, he says, surprised. And I've always liked the name Italo for a boy.

Hmm, says Carmen. I won't breastfeed, so you and the baby will have a chance to bond via the feeding experience.

I could be a superior househusband, he says doubtfully. Griffin doesn't know anything about children. Neither does his mother. Fran wrinkles her nose in disgust at the masturbation stains on his bed when she changes the sheets.

Anyway, how can they live together, let alone get married; it's a great big joke what with both of them still

8

in school and no real money to live on except from rotten summer jobs, landscaping for Griffin and waitressing for Carmen.

There is always more opportunity for sex in the summer, though, since the warm weather lets them use the car or the shelter of trees in city parks. Their bones clash rhythmically in the dark, bodies pale and pasted together, a four-legged, two-headed amoeba. Because they have no privacy, they rely on masturbatory short cuts, their uniforms clothes that fall open but stay on. Most of all, they rely on speed. Carmen scuttles for cover when headlights peer through the dripping windshield, or the beam of a flashlight skips through the trees. She is an expert at pulling her jeans up, or her skirt down, her cheeks bright red but her mouth bland and virginal, her hair, the colour of blades of wheat, falling smoothly into place. Griffin just takes a flip to his fly, lies serenely in the half-dark of the car seat, or propped against a tree trunk, arms crossed behind his head, his skin opal.

It's not like we're committing a crime, says Carmen. Next time we should just keep going. Too bad for whoever walks in on us.

One day they will live together like a real couple. Not necessarily get married, Carmen sees marriage as territorial and possessive. Why, once she tried to find a married friend in the phone book and couldn't because she didn't know the husband's last name.

Sometimes bits of gravel and dust on the floor of Griffin's parents' car get stuck in her underpants. One day she will stop lying and tell her parents she and Griffin are spending the night together. She will just *tell* them.

Screwing in a car and getting gravel in her pants is preferable to winter sex. Winters they have to resort to a dangerous game of tag with Fran, grabbing sex in whatever room of the house they're sure she's not in. If she's upstairs they skitter downstairs to the room with the pool table, or the laundry room. If she's downstairs they spill their juices in his bedroom (not on the bed, for God's sake — the springs! the springs!) or on the kitchen floor, or upright in the dark front hallway. What can they do, they're so much in love, the urge just takes them and they can't help themselves.

For now, since it's summer, they use Fran and Godfrey's car floor, Carmen's parents' car, Fish Creek park, or if they're lucky, her best friend Joan's apartment. Do it on top of a sleeping bag on the living room floor. Carmen gets nervous about having sex in other people's beds. Profane somehow. Embarrassing when there's a mess.

Carmen works mostly the morning shifts and then leaves for home in the middle of the afternoon. Her uniform is a pair of navy blue cotton shorts with a white cotton shirt and an apron she folds over and ties around her waist. She carries menus in her left hand, swiftly pours coffee with her right, and can carry up to six full plates of food at a time. Most days she combs her hair into an orderly ponytail, barrettes the sides so the long straight strands don't drag in the food, and sprays her bangs until they crackle. If she wakes up early enough she can French-braid her hair, spray it, then curl the bangs into a springy slope across her forehead. Ringlets are her favourite, ringlets on both sides of her face, and her back hair in a bun. She looks dynamite with ringlets, Griffin says so, the other waitresses say so, *Carmen* says so, but ringlets drag in the plates of food and by the end of a shift have transformed into long, greasy, eggy, jam-encrusted strands tucked behind her ears anyway. Bangs scraped back and a bun at the back of the head are the most sanitary way to go, but really, what is she? A nurse? Or worse, a nun? She has to feel proud of herself.

The more tables she has the more challenged she feels, the better she performs; she moves with figure-skating speed and grace as she whirls out coffee, menus, food, keeps her customers happy, and chatters in a friendly but business-like manner.

White or brown? Apple or orange? Overeasy or sunnyside up? Cash or charge?

She is, undoubtedly, the best waitress in the world. But being the best waitress isn't necessarily the best career choice.

Waitressing is the job she resigns herself to every summer. Every year she swears she'll find a job more suitable to her area of university study, a job less demeaning, a job less *high schoolish.*

We have unlimited potential! she insists to Griffin. We can do better than this!

But the wage improves every year and so does she; she has to be realistic. She will keep waitressing until she is offered a better-paying, more meaningful alternative. This year her manager, Rama, is a woman, originally from India or somewhere, and so sensitive. Rama unbalances all the waitresses, not only because she is so strict but also because she is the most beautiful woman in the world.

You know, says Luce, a waitress who's been at the restaurant even longer than Carmen, these Pakistani-types have such beautiful complexions. Smooth as babies' butts. And big brown puppy eyes to boot. Amazing.

Uh-huh, says Carmen.

Although, you know, continues Luce, my second cousin's married to a man who's black as the ace of spades and his complexion isn't the greatest, I have to say. So some of these coloured people don't have the best skin. Rama has beautiful skin. She's one of the lucky ones.

Uh-huh.

Because what else is there to say. Carmen is afraid to say anything else, she has never worked so closely with a coloured person before. Rama even smells different. Spicy, or flowery, some strange brown-skin perfume. The distinctly gritty smell of powdered armpits when Rama sweats. She's seen Rama spread hand lotion on. Standard hand lotion. It's the chemistry of a person's skin, she's heard, that can make a perfume change its smell. Rama must have a certain chemical makeup to make her body smell this way with just a bit of hand lotion. Or maybe it's what Rama eats at home, although Rama eats restaurant food just like everyone else during breaks. She's heard

13

East Indians eat a lot of curry in their food. Is it curry? Carmen likes curry. Maybe it's just the combination of hand lotion and brown skin and sweat. Pigment transforming smell.

Carmen has known few coloured women, so Rama makes her nervous; she would never ask Rama what she eats at home or what perfume she wears. All the coloured women Carmen meets seem so *angry*, not that Carmen's ever met any really — well she's been in the same classes as some but they don't seem to talk very much generally. She's seen them on television at demonstrations and riots and things in the United States. Always in packs. Carmen is afraid to speak in front of Rama, afraid she might say something that will offend. What if Carmen causes a riot by saying something racist? Carmen knows how different races stick together, she's seen ethnic gangs on the news.

Rama's hair, long shiny black hair cut so perfect and make-up matched to her skin. Carmen tells Griffin that Rama's skin is like cinnamon, or no, cappuccino. Carmen would like a tan halfway between her own skin colour and Rama's. This would be the perfect colour.

Customers naturally ask Rama where she comes from, and Rama says "CANADA" like she's offended. Carmen and the other waitresses hang out in the kitchen, gossip and flirt with the prep cooks whenever Rama's out of the way. Rama's too uptight, she'll never last, they say. Is she even qualified to be a restaurant manager? Heard she's sleeping with the owner.

Get your asses back to work, yells the chef, he's a grouchy little man, and the prep cooks mutter about how they work their asses off, work like niggers, do most of the work in fact— why's a Chinese guy cooking *hamburgers* anyway? Stick to egg foo yung at the Long Duck Dong.

Yeah, Long Duck Dong, Long Duck's Dong, Duck's Long Dong, echo the waitresses, and they scatter. Carmen doesn't ever say this out loud, but Duck's Long Dong is what pops into her head whenever the chef screws up an order. Long Dong Duck. Long Duck Dong.

Norm, yells Luce. I can't serve this bacon! This bacon's still squealing!

Luce skewers the bacon on the small plate with a fork, takes a bite out of it.

Maybe in China people are happy with raw meat, but welcome to the Western world!

Norm pushes a small plate of bacon towards Luce, doesn't speak, only keeps cooking, sweat dripping from his forehead, soaking into the rim of his chef's hat.

Stick to making chop suey, mutters Luce. Ching chong duck damn dong. She pops a slice of butter on her plate of food.

What did you say? says Rama.

Nothing, I didn't say anything. Just talking to Norm.

What did you say?

Nothing. Jesus.

Rama goes into her office and closes the door. Luce serves her customers their breakfasts, passes the office on the way to the coffee station.

Rama opens the door slightly and gestures to Luce with a long, shiny fingernail, the inside of her finger pink and the outside dark, coffee-flavoured brown. The office door closes behind them.

Carmen and the other waitresses do their jobs, keep their ears toward the office door in case either Luce or Rama say something loud enough to penetrate. The waitresses change ashtrays that contain only a smidgen of ash, pour coffee for their tables over and over until customers become annoyed by the excessive attention. Could I have the bill, miss, please? I don't need any more coffee.

Carmen's bangs droop and feather into her face from the nervous sweat on her forehead. She takes over Luce's tables.

Luce stays in Rama's office until the restaurant is closed. Luce's voice pierces through the door, shrill and constant. The waitresses cluster, waiting for their tips to be collected and distributed. They stand close to the office door, but not too close in case either Rama or Luce behind the door lash out and burn them.

Luce steps out of the office and closes the door behind her. She stands facing the other waitresses, swaying a little, her face carved from wax. She stands and sways under the fluorescent lighting of the restaurant, her skin shiny from sweat and oil, her lipstick bitten off and the exposed skin on her lips chapped and raw. Luce's body suddenly shrinks, crouches as she gathers breath into her lungs. She screams. Screams and screams and screams, her face blossoming into a bright and rabid pink. She twirls around and gives Rama's door the violent middle finger of her right hand, then her left hand, then kicks the fake wooden panelling, left foot, right foot, left foot, right foot.

Everyone says that, shrieks Luce between kicks, everyone does! We say it to his face, he doesn't mind, he likes it, he's used to it! What does he expect coming to this country, that he'll *fit in*? I was going to quit this job anyway! You wouldn't know how to run a fucking restaurant if your fucking life depended on it!

Luce holds a pink slip, the same colour as her face. Blood gone from her knuckles, she crumples the slip in her hand, and throws it on the floor. Rama doesn't answer, doesn't even watch Luce run out of the restaurant and down the street still in her uniform, just opens the door to her office then sits back down behind her desk.

Rama counts out the waitresses' tips into even piles of ten-, five-, two-dollar bills and loonies with her dark brown fingers, her fingernails polished and pinky-brown as sea-shells on a tropical beach. Her fingernails brush and tap the surface of her desk. The door to the office now wide open, Carmen and the other waitresses line up at Rama's desk, listen to the fine clicks of her fingernails, the snap of money in her hands. Rama counts out money, writes down numbers, lightly swivels her body in her chair as she reaches from one part of the desk to the other. The waitresses stand around the desk in a semicircle, simmering, resentful, afraid. Rama lifts her face, wrings them all dry with a *look.*

Carmen's stomach sinks whenever Rama approaches her, whenever Rama swishes past, long black hair spread fan-like across her shoulders, make-up always dark and perfect. Rama the thundercloud. She tells Carmen not to forget to water table eight, or that table one needs their ashtray changed — as if Carmen needs someone to tell her how to do her job. Carmen speaks to Rama not at all if she can help it.

Hi Rama, 'bye Rama. This is all she would say if she could get away with it.

The prep cooks, one by one, are replaced.

Not too busy today, eh, says Rama.

No. No it's not, says Carmen. She looks down to make sure her apron's on straight. She left a little note for Rama asking for tomorrow off, she hopes and prays that Rama will give her tomorrow off, tomorrow Griffin has promised to take her to the mountains.

Guess we won't be needing you tomorrow morning then. Hasn't been too busy lately.

Thanks!

Carmen feels a tear-pricking surge of gratitude and fondness for Rama. Carmen wants to hug Rama until she cracks. Rama smiles.

Where do you come from Rama? Carmen ventures,

feeling chummy and happy. I mean originally you know?

Well, Rama hesitates, I was born in Winnipeg. That's where my parents come from.

Rama isn't so frightening after all, maybe they could even be friends.

Winnipeg. Well. I guess I mean where does your family really come from. My boyfriend's Scottish all the way back and his dad even has a *kilt* stashed away. You speak without an accent, just like you're Canadian. You know, with Canadian parents.

The air around Rama's body glints polished slate. Carmen, unable to stop, finds herself saying: You're not like other coloured people of course. You don't *act* coloured. A lot of the time I don't even notice. Your skin, I mean. Maybe it's none of my business.

Maybe it's not, answers Rama softly.

I'm sorry. But I don't understand, I don't understand what the big deal is. I mean we're all the same underneath aren't we? I would never say anything racist intentionally, but wouldn't it be better for me to know just in case I make a mistake? Why can't you just tell me why it bugs you so much when people ask you where you come from? Why are you so angry all the time? What d'you have against white people anyway? This isn't a racist town, it's not like the KKK goes galloping up and down the streets or something. You've got a good job. I don't know why people have to be so sensitive all the time. Why not just integrate? Why try to stick out all the time? People don't mean to be mean. Surely you understand *that.* Don't set yourself up as a target — be more casual.

The sound of her own voice sounds off-key to Carmen, too high or too low, strings snapped from a violin under a rigidly-applied bow. The words that come from her mouth don't belong to anyone she knows. Belong to the other, another Carmen.

Carmen sees Rama's hands start to shake, the blood rush to Rama's face, Rama's mouth about to say something, something, but her voice eclipsed by Carmen's questions. Carmen sounds like a drunk person, slurs her words in a tipsy monologue.

Educate me, says Carmen. Show me where all this racism is, why you're so angry and bitchy all the time. Show me. If I cut you you bleed, if I cut me I bleed, we're all the same underneath. Show me the difference. Show me the difference!

Carmen's lips can't stop stretching and singing: Luce calling Norm Long Duck Dong is the same as you calling us Canucks. Being called a Canuck may hurt my feelings but I don't let it get to me. I have other more important problems.

Carmen flinches at the backfire crack in Rama's back, Carmen having laid on the last precious straw and at last, Carmen is going to lose her job, she's going to end up like Luce, broke and with no reference and her work history ruined. Now she won't be able to pay for school and she'll have to ask her parents for money and they'll want to know why and what if they don't have enough money to put her through school this year? She'll have to take out a loan, she knows all about loans, her cousin Josepha got a loan and she's *still* paying for it, twenty-five thousand dollars in debt and only twenty-six years old. Carmen closes her eyes. I am not going to cry I am not going to cry dear God please don't let me cry, dear God please don't let me lose this job I'll do anything, and she prays oh she prays even though she doesn't believe in God, up until now she hasn't believed in anything anything anything. Her mouth opens and closes, opens and closes, her instrument wound to the breaking point.

Three veins in Rama's forehead stretch upward in the shape of a trident. She gives Carmen a *look,* but this time the look pulls apart Carmen's face, peels off Carmen's skin. *I cut you you bleed I cut me I bleed,* burrows through the layer of subcutaneous fat and splays out her veins and nerves, frayed electrical wires, snaps apart Carmen's muscles and scrapes at Carmen's bones, digs and gouges away Carmen's life.

The colour of Carmen's pink and freckled fingers and forearms deepens, darkens to freckled chocolate brown and beige pink on the palms of her hands. Her hair curls and frizzes, shortens. Hairs dropped into a frying pan kink up around her face, curl into tight balls on the back of her neck. Her skin, covered in a thin layer of dry skin, flakes from where she missed with the skin lotion this morning. Her hair is drier, finer; irises freshly dipped in dark brown cradle her pupils. And her scars, old knotted scars from childhood, from last year, from last week when she touched the hot oven with the back of her hand, open their eyes and glare pale against her skin. Her history is etched out in negative.

The hot slab of granite that is Rama's face dissolves as Carmen changes and Rama suddenly laughs. Laughs and says, Yeah, some of my best friends are coloured people too. I even know some okay white people. And Carmen lets out a breath.

Carmen, now a brown girl, keeps her job *and* gets tomorrow off to go to the mountains with her one true love.

Carmen also starts to laugh, the bridges of the two women's noses wrinkle meanly as they laugh, and Carmen goes back to her station. Waters the customers and fetches more buns and whipped butter from the kitchen to stop the rumbles of hunger, the questions: Where do you come from? How long you been in Canada? Is the seafood here fresh?

23

Part of the job, part of the job, the customer is always right.

One of these days, I swear Rama, Carmen says, I'm going to give these dumb white people what-for.

This is how metamorphoses work. They happen all the time. Women turn into trees, birds, flowers, disembodied voices at the moment of crisis, just before anger, grief, desperation eats them alive. Daphne twists and stumbles away from Apollo until she gnarls into a tree, her smooth skin rough and impenetrable, forever a virgin. Echo's love unrequited, she withers into her name. Loses herself to love instead of cutting her losses and finding a new lover. Other fish in the sea — she should have asked to be a trout instead. Women who've lost their mothers grow poplar bark and weep sap, as though tears of sugar instead of salt make the sadness less. Or attractively more. The more charming you are in your sadness the more likely you can be saved. The more desperate the more likely you will be saved. Take a second look and become a pillar of salt.

At the most horrible moment bodies transform into bears, nightingales, bats. But which bodies? Who's so lucky? White girls in a blasted moment grow the bark and flow with the sap of coloured girls. But this is only one moment.

25

I've never seen lips on a vagina so brown, says Griffin. I've never touched black hair, can I touch it? So soft.

Stupid question, Carmen says. What a stupid question.

Well you know what they say, says Griffin, as he strokes her black black hair, pushes in her dark brown nipples. Once you sleep with a black, you never go back. Something like that.

Carmen and Griffin cover their mouths with their hands, giggle at his naughtiness.

I've always wanted to sleep with a black woman.

Oh yeah? Why's that?

But she is more concerned that he is leaving, going to Europe, than she is about her new *pelt*, as Griffin calls it. Her *pelt*, he says and strokes the skin all over her body. She knows Griffin has always wanted to travel to Europe, *has* to. It's his dream, he's planned to go all his life, still it's hard not to want him to stay with her, it's hard to give him up for so long. She thought of going, long ago when he first mentioned Europe, but he never *asked* her.

Of course she never asked him to ask her. Her priorities are different. What's the big deal anyway, meet more people, meet more problems. She works in the public service field — she knows. And money. What about the money? She wants to finish school first, she's not a stupid girl. Europe is all fine and dandy but afterwards, then what?

It's the experience, Griffin always says. I want to see other places, other people. Get a better sense of how I fit in the world. See Buckingham Palace before I settle down.

One of them has to be practical, experience won't pay the rent, won't free them from living in their parents' houses. She doesn't mind being the practical one. If they both went to Europe they couldn't afford to move in together until they were both in their fifties! She loves Griffin, but sometimes he can be so unmotivated, so short-sighted, so live-for-the-moment.

Don't spend all your money over there, she pleads, Save some for when you get back, remember our moving-in-together fund!

Maybe his spontaneity is why she loves him, so different from herself. She'll miss him so much, like having plant roots ripped out of her soil.

Do you love me? she asks.

Of course.

If you love me then why are you going to Europe?

Umm. Uhh.

She sees the sweat spring out on his forehead as he scampers in his little brain for an answer. Poor sweet thing.

I'm just kidding, she says. Just testing.

They walk in the park together, hand in hand. She admires her long brown legs in the sun, smells the lemon-scented laundry detergent of her clean cotton t-shirt. She puts her arm around his waist. A beautiful day. *They* are not as beautiful as usual, though, she isn't wearing make-up today. Hasn't worn make-up for almost two weeks, her make-up from before no longer fits her brown skin. She never realized how vital make-up is to making a girl feel good about herself. Just a little something to brighten up her face, her heart. She even catches herself avoiding mirrors now. But at least she has Griffin, and Griffin doesn't seem to mind her naked face. Griffin thinks she's beautiful no matter what. He is wearing the nice blue shirt she bought him last Christmas, one hundred percent cotton. She slides her hand under the shirt, feels the indented small of his moist back, the shifting muscles with each step. Notices how people stare.

Haven't you noticed? she asks. Strange isn't it?

I guess that's because we're a mixed couple now, he says. Just like John Lennon and Yoko Ono. He squeezes her hand. He's so smart.

I guess we'll have cocoa babies, he says and Carmen smiles, she has always liked the look and smell of cocoa. Hot chocolate is her favourite drink. Hot chocolate in winter, chocolate milk in summer. Small brown babies, hers and Griffin's. Maybe if they have a boy, the baby's middle name could be Italo.

Pushing her little chocolate Italo in a carriage through the park.

Fran fries up dinner, sprinkles in dried parsley and juice from a plastic lemon. Frowns a little when Griffin walks into the kitchen, no doubt with Carmen in tow. But Fran thinks busily of other things, Godfrey and his biological research in Mexico (don't drink the water!), her now full-time secretarial job. Fran has been married for too long. She and the New Boss — he was the "new" boss when they first met — have been seeing each other regularly for a long time now and, lately, God doesn't even seem to care any more — this is how long they've been married. Today when she and the New Boss closed themselves in his office and began kissing and stroking and kissing and stroking, they ended up kissing and stroking and mewling and loving a little too insistently and she banged her wedding ring against his desk so hard the stones gouged the wood, then dropped out. She sustained a bone bruise on the finger, but no blood bubbled from the scratched skin. Fran knew this was a bad sign, a warning sign, a sign from God. She did not get down on her knees to search for the missing jewels, she did not think they were worth the risk of bumping her head on the corner of the desk, of maybe even cutting herself.

Fran remembers the time she saw a woman bump her head so hard the bump nearly killed her. An old woman hit by a car and sitting on the curb in front of Fran's house. Fran didn't see the accident, but a man came to the door and asked Fran's mother if he could use the phone, there'd been an accident. A woman hit by a car. Fran looked out the window — she'd been arranging peonies in a vase in the front hall — and saw the woman, an old, old woman sitting on the curb and supported by strangers, dropped on the curb exactly in front of Fran's mother's house. Through the bevelled glass in the front window Fran saw the blood bubble up then pour and pour from the old woman's head, and was surprised because she didn't know that old people bled, always assumed that they were full of something else, sand maybe. Sand is what she is afraid could pour from her own head.

The New Boss gets down on his knees though, searches and searches for the missing stones, his tight little bum high up in the air. It's as though the diamonds have turned into drops of water, soaked into the carpet.

Don't worry, she says. It's God's will, she says. She pats him on the rump, then the head, then the rump.

Fran and the New Boss love each other a little more, mewl and paw on the little foam pad the New Boss keeps rolled away in his desk. They are oblivious to the stones buried in the carpet under their pad, Fran's sharp and rocky signs from God, and the New Boss puts on a condom. Fran and the New Boss and the condom do it in his inner office so hard the New Boss's face turns red then purple, his head splits apart, the sections of an orange, and Fran's grey poodle hair gets pushed and ruffled into a macaw's crown.

The phone rings just as they finish intercourse, and Fran finds the New Boss's head and her own head just in time to reconnect them and scramble to the phone, buttoning up the front of her dress, readjusting her breasts in their brassiere cups. The New Boss sits behind his desk, watches Fran and smiles like an imp when she hands the phone to him, who else would it be for? This is their private joke. He looks just like one of those gnome lawn ornaments. The ring and its empty claws lost in the bottom of her purse.

When Fran and God perform intercourse, her head disconnects, but this decapitation is because she is a disinterested wife. She admits her failure as God's spouse. If her life had been up to her she would never have married so young, certainly never chosen God for a husband. In her heart she is a free agent. Those wedding vows were for her mother more than herself. And God's head is always connected, God's head never splits apart in ecstasy, God would never lose control and clutch her by the shoulders the way the New Boss does. It's almost as though God feels he is doing his duty, satisfying the desire he thinks she undoubtedly must have after waiting for him all those months while he's doing his research, top secret, highly classified governmental research, she knows his work involves looking at musk oxen faeces or some such thing. She realizes this work is important — he's told her; she's figured out his status in the faeces field from all the dinners given in his honour, all the research trips he makes, the guest lectures he's invited to give. She tries to show she's proud of him, she gets her hair done for him, but he rarely notices her efforts, hardly cares about her life, why should she care back? Really she could go without having sex with God ever again. Sex with God is as exciting as reheating leftovers. But this is old news, shut up in an old shoe box in her head.

Griffin caught them once when he was ten years old, walked into their bedroom for who knows what reason, then walked right out again — a perfect one hundred and eighty degree turn. She wanted to shout at Griffin to come back in, but her body collapsed from embarrassment, waited poised for the moment when Griffin would ask her what she and Daddy were doing.

Having a nap, was her answer. Now finish your hamburger.

Fran grunts under God's white and curly weight, his breath in her face, on her neck. When her head reconnects it is nothing but a vessel for bland and familiar shame. She drinks shame out of their expensive crystal glasses, polishes it off the taps in the newly renovated bathroom. She was never taught to enjoy her body, had to teach herself. God certainly doesn't appear to enjoy her body, he enjoys looking at other women's bodies she's noticed, and she's sure he has women lolling around naked on the sidelines. Her mother didn't give her practical, sensible advice when Fran needed to know about penises. Just gave Fran an embroidered handkerchief, a blue silk hair ribbon to include in her bridal headpiece, a penny for her shoe. Something borrowed, something blue, and a penny in your shoe. How about some real money, enough money for a down payment on a house, who cares about a rotten penny? Instead of a goddamn hanky how about a borrowed wedding-night sex manual and a vibrator, even though vibrators didn't exist in those days? Fran accidentally discovered the multiple uses of the back massager several years into her marriage. The massager dropped into her lap and from that day forward she valued no household appliance more.

Fran angrily uses the bidet to clean her shame and dabs herself down below quickly and efficiently with a towel she throws impatiently down the laundry chute. Out of sight.

34

Fran stirs up dinner, sees the girl holding Griffin's hand for only a second, this girl sticking her tongue in Griffin's ear, but that's enough. That's enough to know Holy Dinah that damn Griffin goddammit to hell Jesus Christ sugar consarnit has gotten out of control, his brain always always between his legs. What is he trying to do? Kill her? Push her in front of a bus with his monstrous insensitivity? This is a thought that has crossed her mind more than a few times.

Where's Carmen? asks Fran. Sweat prickles her fore-head and rivers, no, oceans of Fran's blood pour into her head. Her hands shake with rage.

This *is* Carmen, says Griffin. Ma, don't be dumb.

Hey Fran, says Carmen, and Carmen ducks her head hello in that evade-the-eye-oh-so-insolent way.

Carmen? says Fran. Oh. Of course. I didn't recognize you.

And Carmen shyly bows her head as though proud of her new accomplishment.

Fran, Carmen, and Griffin eat fried liver and onions at Fran's long dining room table.

Potato salad? Carmen? asks Fran. The girl across the table, the girl who used to be Carmen, who even in some strange way *looks* like Carmen, nods insolently just like the old Carmen used to do. But this is not Carmen. This is not the Carmen Fran can know and tolerate. This is not the Carmen Fran has been trying to shape into an appropriate vessel for her grandchild. This is no one Fran knows, no one she wants to know. The black girl sitting across from Fran, the black girl also named Carmen, nods in the direction of the potato salad again, just as contemptuously as the old Carmen used to, and Fran whips the bowl of potato salad across the table.

Griffin slices up liver into tiny bits and hides them under slices of fried onion, macaroni casserole, lettuce leaves. Carmen thinks only one more month and the university semester will start, only two more weeks and then Griffin, her lover, her man, goes to Europe and she won't see him for eight whole months! Tears in her eyes, in her nose. She's dreadfully afraid she's going to start crying at the table. Her vision hideously impaired by all the tears, Carmen keeps her face down over her plate of liver. Bathes her hot cheeks in the steam. Doesn't notice Fran's little round eyes taking aim and firing at the black girl sitting at her table where no black girl has ever sat.

Fran remembers when she was five. She remembers spinning in delirious circles watching her skirt spread out around her, the petals of an opening flower. She runs up and down the hallway in the back of the church, turns her head to watch the ribbons streaming from her hair, she swings and swings her empty basket, soon to be filled with rose petals until her mum taps her on the head, shushes her with a Can't you be still? and raised eyebrows. Fran the flower girl crouches on the floor, the cream taffeta skirt balloons around her, she pretends she is an upside-down mushroom, her torso and head the stem.

The bride, Mabel, swaddled in antique lace and silk, makes her entrance, her father holding her arm, her face hidden under layers and layers of white, water clouded with milk. Fran's basket is filled with rose petals, her hair given one last comb, her pink sash tightened, she is pushed out by an usher into the aisle between the pews. Handfuls of red petals, white petals, pink petals, Fran walks and scatters the petals evenly and slowly as she was instructed, scatters the petals over the velvety red runner. She reaches the front of the church, puffs out her cheeks and sits next to her mum in one of the front pews. Mabel's head is bowed under the veils, her hand in the crook of her father's arm, his face stern and royal. He's glad he's finally got his only daughter out of the way, took some manoeuvring, some would even call it blackmail, but blackmail, that's a dirty word, no place for such a word at a wedding, but now maybe she'll be a little more manageable, what with a husband and babies to take care of. He knows there'll be lots of babies, he had a long talk with the groom earlier, guaranteed the groom a job at his bank once the first baby was born. The bride's mother sobs in gratitude, thanking her lucky stars, thanking God, that she and her least favourite child, her daughter with the tongue of a viper and the morals of a mongrel bitch, will no longer have to live under the same roof, thanking God her daughter will now be tamed and controlled at last, safely out of the way. Mabel talking back to her father, chain-smoking at the dinner table, wanting to travel instead of marry, have a job instead of be a wife. Mabel's outlandish suggestion that he spend his money on medical school for her instead of a wedding reception. Mabel's mother wishes Mabel would just keep quiet, keep her thoughts and her crass, booming voice to herself. In a tiny corner of her heart, Mabel's mother pities the groom, but this is something she would never never admit, not even if she were tortured, not even if she were confronted by a pride of wild man-eating lions. And, oh, at last she will have grandchildren, many many grandchildren! She hopes Mabel's children are as evil to Mabel as Mabel has been to her.

Mabel hands her bouquet to the Maid of Honour. The Maid of Honour's coarse, short hair straggles from the flowered comb at the back of her head. The Maid of Honour holds the bouquet nonchalantly, as though she wouldn't care if it dropped and all the beautiful blush-coloured roses came tumbling out to be stepped on. The seams of the Maid's stockings, Fran notices, are crooked and her hair-style is vastly unbecoming to her — long, big ears, pointy even, exposed because the hair is pulled back, just like all the attendants' hair. Fran watches the Maid of Honour fidget, toes tapping, heels clicking together, the muscles of her calves flexing. The Maid of Honour shifts the bouquet to her right arm, her left arm pats the back of her hair and tries to readjust an errant bobby pin. But for all her fidgeting, the Maid of Honour is diligent; she grimly straightens Mabel's train, pulls out the wrinkles while clutching the bouquet securely, struggles not to crunch the delicate lace gloves Mabel hands her when it's time for the exchange of rings. The Maid of Honour fusses quietly, snickers and rolls her eyes when the groom mixes up the order of Mabel's middle names, stifles a laugh when she sees his hands shake while he holds the ring. She shifts impatiently from one foot to the other as though commenting with her body on the progress of the ceremony. A botched and stupid affair, her body suggests, the groom a big dolt, the whole ceremony a waste of her time. She lifts her fingers clumsy and paw-like when she smooths out the veil that the groom has drawn back from his new wife's face, ready to kiss her, Mabel, the perfect bride. The Maid of Honour watches the groom lick his lips with his gross, pink tongue in preparation for the kiss. Her face scrunches up as she bursts out with an exasperated whinny and a toss of her hair. The comb of flowers falls from her head as she falls to her hands and knees; her exposed skin sprouts a thick layer of fur. Mabel catches the bouquet as it falls, and both she and the groom step back as the Maid of Honour's hips and bust split out from the dress, her neck thickens, her face grows longer and her eyes widen in surprise. The Maid of Honour's hooves burst from her satin-covered pumps and she lifts up her hooves and sets them down clop-clopping in the restricted space between the altar and the pews. The Maid of Honour rears up on her hind legs and snorts, her front hooves fall heavily to the polished wood and expensive carpeting, her tail swishes back and forth violently. She rams between Mabel and the groom, stomps on Mabel's train, rips away Mabel's veil with her teeth and chews it.

Easy does it, says Mabel, easy does it. Mabel reaches out a trembling hand and rests it on the horse's side. The horse's mouth swings towards Mabel's ear, her horsy lips whisper and nicker.

Mabel lets out a whoop, hikes up the skirt of her gown and jumps on the Maid's back, her legs smooth and lovely next to the rough dark coat. Mabel's headpiece slides to the back of her head and she tosses the bouquet into the congregation. The two women gallop from the church, ribbons and lace streaming behind. Fran lets out a whoop, the guests and relatives let out screams of surprise and the groom's father's face turns purple with rage. His son dumped at the altar! All that money lost!

The groom's mother buries her face in her corsage and smiles so hard she is afraid she will faint. The groom drops his face into his hands and tears seep out from the corners of his eyes, not from sadness but from the sweet shock of relief.

Kidnapping! shrieks the priest. Kidnapping!

The lips of the bride's father purse in violent irritation, or his lips would purse together if he had any lips — he's not an attractive man, he's the kind of man who barges to the front of line-ups because his business is always more important than other people's business — his lips form a bloodless slash in the bottom half of his face, a slice in the rind of a juiceless melon.

Maybe he can get some of his money back. Mabel better not come asking for money or his forgiveness because the answer is a flat out NO.

Mabel's mother wonders whether any of the other guests have brought along smelling salts because she is about to pretend to faint. She assumes fainting is the correct behaviour for the mother of a run-away bride. The wedding etiquette books say nothing about this kind of situation. She wonders what will happen to the wedding dress, oh well, she won't have a granddaughter to pass it on to so it doesn't matter. She falls onto the soft carpet, her arms spread out, and closes her eyes. Any minute now someone will notice her and she can go home to bed and never get up again.

Once she's safely away, Mabel removes the penny from her shoe and bores a hole in it. She wears the penny on a string around her neck for continued good luck, and braids the ribbons and flowers from her hair into Honour's glossy mane.

Shouldn't Carmen be going home soon, says Fran. Shouldn't she be leaving? It's getting late. She clears up the dishes still full of steak tartar — of course Griffin hasn't eaten any. Fran thought that maybe she'd cook something a little special since he's leaving in three days, and Carmen, well Carmen eats like a horse, she'll pay for it when she's older. Fran knows from TV that the older black women get, the bigger their butts and hips. Once Griffin comes back from Europe, Carmen will no longer be invited for dinners.

Fran has taken to referring to Carmen in the third person now, sometimes ignoring her entirely when she's in the room. Fran's eyes avoid the space Carmen occupies, it's too awful to see her; all she can think of is that stupid, foul-mouthed Oprah Winfrey and her fat, flat face.

Hair like a golliwog's, thinks Fran. All of this Carmen can hear now that she's a brown girl and sensitive to these things, sensitive to the slurs Fran throws at Carmen with her body, her eyes. Carmen can tell when Fran tries to erase her, bury her under images of Buckwheat and old toy golliwogs. Carmen thinks loudly, you always were a dumb cunt anyway Fraaan, may your husband be fucking one of his male employees right now. Carmen shouts this into the biggest megaphone she can imagine but all Fran hears is the buzz of a fly bumping against the window.

Griffin walks with Carmen to the car to kiss her good-bye. See you tomorrow, he says. Hugs and kisses her then hugs and kisses her and wrinkles his forehead at her wet wet eyes.

One more time before you go? Carmen asks. Sniffs. She winds a finger in her short, stiff ponytail.

He lets his arm dangle out the window as they drive to the park. He wonders if he should return his plane ticket. This thought has occurred to him again and again. Eight months is a long time to be away. A faint, distorted echo of this thought will return to him when he is in Portugal, watching Renata from Spain wipe his semen off her stomach with his t-shirt. Return his plane ticket? And miss this? Renata smells like ferns in the rain.

How can anyone know what might have been, says Renata. All I know is what is. Bodies and pleasure, she says. Foucault, Grrrriffin. Or should I call you Italo?

This is how Renata talks. In real life.

Carmen and Griffin have goodbye sex in the back seat of the car and take all their clothes off because of the sad special occasion. Carmen's eyes rivet to their bodies, she's never seen them together naked, they are almost never naked together, not like this, not completely naked. She can't keep her eyes off their bodies. Their shifting chessboard pattern. Griffin's skin suddenly so pale, so *white* and her skin so brown, so *black* in the diffused light. Their bodies two ropes of contrasting colours twined then falling apart and braided together then falling apart again. She rubs his chest, spreads her fingers out across his rib cage, confused by the colour contrast between his ribs, her fingers.

Their hips gnash together, the teeth of a nervous sleeper, but their skeletons always apart, separated by layers of skin, fat and blood. The same underneath? Just bones. Maybe not.

Headlights sweep through the car but neither of them move to retrieve their clothes. Carmen is ready for Griffin to leave now. Everything will be all right.

The night before he leaves, Griffin says that Carmen can't see him off at the airport.

What? she says. What?

My mother wants to see me off. She says she'll be there to see me off no matter what. You can't see me off. She wants to be the one there when her only son leaves.

What? What are you talking about? What does your *mother* have to do with us? Who gives a shit what she thinks? Why are you listening to her? To *her*? I'm the one you love! Why can't we both be there to see you off?

Carmen howls, her mouth wide and deep. Fran that bleached gob of DOG SHIT!

I love you, Carmen, says Griffin, his voice quiet. I'm sorry. I don't know what's wrong with her. Why she thinks she has to be there alone.

Ma, says Griffin, Carmen's going to see me off at the airport.

Fran begins to cry. She never suspected this could happen, she never knew her son could be so cold-blooded. No, no, she knew this would happen, she knew it would come down to this, the little brain-between-his-legs!

What? Fran says. What are you saying? No, she holds up her hand, Don't say anything, I know what you're saying, I know what you're saying. You're saying you'd rather have some stranger at the airport see you off than your own flesh and blood. You only have one mother, Griffin, only one mother, you'll never have another one. I hope you remember that when you're looking down on my dead face. I'm the one who gave birth to you, I am your blood, she's nothing but a stranger. No, don't touch me, I don't want you at my funeral!

No. Ma. Look, I want you at the airport. Carmen's going to be there, that's all I'm saying!

Well I don't want to go to the airport, says Fran. I don't want to go. Tears dribble out from the pool of salt water housed inside her face, sand from an egg-timer. I won't go. I don't see why you have to go to Europe anyway.

I love you Mom. I'm sorry. I don't know what's wrong with Carmen. Why she thinks she has to be there too.

And that's that. Griffin shoulders his huge backpack, checks for his passport, tickets and money and sees himself off, off to Europe, alone.

The next night he phones Carmen from Rome in tears, the hotel was closed when he arrived, he couldn't find a place to stay, no one speaks English, and Carmen cries also so that the phone becomes damp and sticky on both ends, remember it's a collect call! I wish I were back with you, he says. I should never have left you.

Eight months will be up before you know it, Carmen says, and I'll be waiting for you. She knows this is the right thing to say. The down in her pillow clumps together from the steady dribbling of her tears.

She wonders if he phoned his mother too. Fran's probably too busy masturbating with an ice cube, a cross burning in the ornamental fireplace, to answer the phone.

Before Griffin left, he and Carmen had their first fight in a long time. Over Fran.

She hates me, says Carmen, her teeth bared, tears gnawing like hungry rats at her eyes, her brain. Your mother hated me before but now she really really hates me. Well I hated her first and I hate her more than she hates me. Your mother isn't up against some rookie. I could win any hating contest.

Griffin uses his sleeve to wipe away the tears and running snot. He puts his arm around Carmen's shoulders and says, It's just taking her some time to get used to you. Your skin. Your new pelt. I mean it was easy for me. I can tell you're still the same inside. I think it's cool. I told you I've always wanted to have a black woman. Black women are sexy.

Have a black woman, Carmen says. You can have leprosy, shit-head, but you can't *have* people. Don't be such a fucking shit-head!

Carmen wants to hit him in the mouth. Lately she gets angry so easily, she's become so sensitive sometimes she can't even stand *herself.* Maybe her skin has something to do with this, making her want to be more violent, making her feel downright raw, maybe she *isn't* the same inside. The difference is more fundamental than pelt. Maybe it's in her blood. Like some sort of virus.

This is their first fight in a long time. She is devastated that they are fighting just before he leaves. She has to be careful that she doesn't drive him away so he won't want to come back.

I'm sorry, she says. She nuzzles his shoulder with her wet, hot face.

Yeah well you know what they say, Griffin says.

No, what *do* they say, says Carmen.

Sleep with a black, change your luck.

Good luck, of course, she says, wanting to hit him in the goddamn mouth goddamn well again.

Of course.

Sometimes Griffin can be so slow.

Carmen goes to school, over-exercises from sheer boredom and loneliness, cries at long distance phone commercials on TV, slow songs on the radio, fusses about her hair which is now the consistency of fine wire. Most often she just scrapes it back into a short crinkly ponytail which people always want her to let down.

You know, they say, without barrettes or elastics. Just *down*. Around your shoulders. Like you used to wear your hair when you weren't working.

One of her friends in aerobics class rips out her elastic and stares, fascinated, at Carmen's head when the hair just stays up in its ponytail shape.

Oh my God, your hair doesn't move!

Her hair doesn't go down any more, her hair

sometimes behaves like a mass of wires and maintains the shape barrettes and elastics force it into — no one seems to understand this.

I told you, Carmen says. It's black hair. Not just the colour black, but black. It's black hair! How much more simple can you get?

Carmen grabs back the elastic. Now eff off, I'm depressed, she says.

She pulls one of Griffin's t-shirts over her sports bra. Pulls a pair of his sports tube socks over her ankles. It is her ritual to wear at least one article of Griffin's clothing every day and to sleep in his shirts — flannel for cold and cotton for warmer nights. She has a pillowcase he used for three months straight and never washed stored under her pillow. Before she goes to sleep or when she's feeling especially low, she breathes in its unwashed hair and body odour, then tucks the pillowcase back into its Ziploc plastic bag. The bag stops the smell from fading as fast.

Sometimes she catches the scent of her old self, her old body, in his clothes, her own sweat, the smell of her white hair and scalp back from when her skin was pink. She sniffs these clothes deeply, but loses the smell the harder she breathes in. Tantalized.

He carries one of her unwashed, oversized t-shirts, full of her aerobics sweat and faint perfume, in his backpack. He wears one of her rings on his right pinky finger — one of the cheaper ones, just in case it gets stolen.

Carmen stretches and snaps her hair-elastic back into her hair, checks her bag for her special stash of lipstick, her talisman against the world, smears some on in the gym's locker - room mirror and smiles. Enchanting.

The morning after she turns into a brown girl, the morning after her talk with Rama, she has a shower as usual in the half-darkness, brushes her teeth and begins to put on her make-up. Base powder, lipstick, blush, mascara and two small blobs of eye shadow. She raises her eyes to the mirror, ready to Q-Tip the eyeshadow into subtle smears along the rims of her eyelids. She turns on the bathroom light.

Sees a clown.

A clown, she thinks, the pink lipstick and patchy beige powder too pale for her face and the blue eyeshadow making her look like an exotic goldfish. She pours baby oil into her right hand and rubs her face, rubs her skin with violent circular motions, blurring the lines and curves decorated with make-up, both hands up to her face until blood shows through her oiled skin, through the coloured swirl of chemicals. The whites of her eyes are bloodshot, peppered with bits of mascara.

No make-up the best choice for now anyway what with Griffin leaving. She will cry so much just before he leaves all her make-up will wash off or streak. Griffin leaving. Griffin leaving. Griffin leaves. She gets down to business. A bit of Vaseline on the lips for moisture, but nothing else. Plain brown Jane, her cheque book ready, her face a brown canvas awaiting inspiration.

She shops through malls for make-up that suits her skin, goes to the regular cosmetic counters and picks through the lipsticks she always wears, the old faithfuls, the once sexy bright reds that now make her lips disappear into her face, the risqué light browns that now look like so much grease. Graduated colours of pink, white-girl candy-coloured toxic pink, that smell of foreign, unfamiliar bodies, pink nipples, blonde armpit hairs. Egg-shell, pale eyeshadows, eyeliners in colours that can never show up on her dark skin.

She rubs lipsticks frantically onto her wrists and the backs of her hands to find a colour that suits her, just one colour that won't make her lips look like they're covered in cake icing. She looks sideways every so often into one of the giant mirrors at the cosmetics counter.

Can I help you? asks a sales clerk. That lipstick suits you perfectly, on sale only seventeen ninety-five.

The cosmetician's hair is bone straight and bottle-blonde, eyes a rich blue rimmed with beige shadow, and her freckled skin as Caucasian as Carmen's used to be, not even as light as Carmen's used to be. Carmen looks at the clerk's face and sees her own face, the way her face used to be. The same light hairs on the upper lip, shadows under the eyes, the smoothly painted lips. The clerk *is* Carmen, back when Carmen could take the mirror for granted, when the mirror was her friend. Sweat oozes down Carmen's back, pools in her armpits. An invisible brown paper bag slips over her head. Carmen bursts into tears, overwhelmed by how ugly and inadequate she is. Carmen is a dark brown ogre, defined by nothing but reflections. Reflected back at herself so many times she can only sink into a corner, her head hidden in her arms. Buried alive in glass.

She doesn't see herself for weeks. She remains inside her head, wanting to poke out her own eyes. Her skin dries up and flakes from neglect, she avoids mirrors. She looks wrong, she looks WRONG.

Two weeks before Griffin's birthday, she walks to the drug store by her house, her black head down as usual. Her shadow bumps and slides over the changing textures of the ground. Road tar, sidewalk concrete, dusty rubber mat, worn broadloom, gritty tiles. She buys a birthday card (write it tonight, send it tomorrow) and a sheet of ten international stamps. She tries to console herself with a small, crinkly package of Oreo cookies from the candy counter and looks up only to pay.

Behind the cashier's head is a poster with a woman's dark brown face: FOR THE WOMAN OF COLOUR.

What's that? asks Carmen, and she points. What does that mean?

Make-up, says the cashier. Make-up for coloured women. Other side of the store. Cosmetics and toiletries.

Carmen pays for the cookies. Rushes through aisles and aisles, a brown mouse in a maze, until she reaches the cosmetics counter and sees in the central lipstick rack, the lipstick rack of honour, a lipstick so deeply red it is brown.

She smears some of the tester on the back of her hand, then smears it on her lips just like her mother told her never to do and looks only at her lips and chin in the tiny mirror on the display.

The lips fit her chin. She edges the tip of her nose into the mirror, then the bridge of her nose, then the pouches under her eyes.

Finally her eyes, a brown so dark they look black. Her full, glossy lips frown because it has been so long since they've formed a smile, because she can see either her lips or her eyes but not both, and she wants to see all of herself.

She stays at the counter for hours, phones her parents from the drugstore and says she'll be home late. She stays until closing.

She will never feel ugly again. The name of the woman at the cash register on the candy counter is Rachel. Rachel works Monday to Friday. Early evening shift.

Rachel, sings Carmen.

You again?

How do I look?

Not too bad, not too bad. Hope you plan on buying that lipstick though. You're not supposed to open sealed lipsticks. There're tester samples for trying out.

Of course I'll buy it. I'll buy the whole store.

I'm not holding my breath.

You're an angel.

That's what my mother tells me.

And Rachel is an angel. Carmen's guardian angel. How many Rachels can you fit on the head of a pin? Never enough.

Griffin writes Carmen every week during the first months, his letters and postcards boring but she reads them through at least four times each. Her favourite says:

I MISS MISS MISS YOU.
GOD I MISS YOU. MISS YOU
EVERY HOUR OF EVERY DAY,
EVERY MINUTE OF EVERY
HOUR. FOUND SOME REALLY
COOL VEGETARIAN CHEESE.
STUFF MADE WITHOUT USING
COW STOMACHS. MISS YOU
GRIFFIN. MISS YOU, GRIFFIN.
CAN'T WAIT TO COME HOME
TO YOU, LOVE GRIFFIN.

She tacks all his letters and postcards up on the wall in her bedroom. Dribbles tears of frustration when she tries to locate where he might be on the map of Europe posted above her bed, what post office box she should send his next letter to. Traces his path with her long brown index finger.

She has never cried so much, never been so much in love. So that when she slides her tongue into Kevin's mouth at the Night Gallery, it's just by accident.

You have beautiful eyes, says Kevin, and she knows this is because she's put on a lot of mascara, Smoked Ebony, and Black Onyx eyeliner which make her eyes look black like nuggets of barbecue coal. The name of her lipstick is Midnight Madness; she blames the lipstick, now smeared on Kevin's mouth, his jaw bone.

She puts her mouth on his Adam's apple. The apple Adam ate was forbidden fruit. Kevin's words travel up the crack between her buttocks and ooze glorious fingers down her forehead, across her cheekbones, her own Adam's apple. She puts her mouth on Kevin's penis, but she doesn't suck or kiss, just lets it rest there. They are both naked, but she and Kevin don't have genital-to-genital contact. That would be unfaithful.

Her hair is unbearable when she gets into situations like this. Better to leave it up. So hard to control. Maybe she should go for braids, or straighten it, or cut it all off.

What about Griffin? he asks.

Well, she says, lifts her lips from his penis, Of course I won't ever tell him about this. You can't either. But you know, she says, I think he'd understand.

You figure?

Kevin makes her a tuna fish sandwich before she goes home, slices it in triangles and pokes ornamental toothpicks into the bread. He belly-dances for her to imaginary music while she eats, his fleshy, naked stomach jiggles and his hips undulate. Kevin smiles fetchingly, runs his fingers over Carmen's shoulders, the back of her neck as she eats, and she giggles because he is tickling. He would never do this for his own girlfriend who doesn't find him that funny. His girlfriend tells him to see a therapist when he wiggles his body in provocative ways.

Carmen would never give up Griffin for Kevin, no question. She and Griffin have too much history, too much invested in each other. And he knew her when she was a white girl. Her white-girl self is a memory she still wants to keep near, immediate, since every day she's remembering less and less of who she once was. She sometimes even forgets why she should remember.

Next time she thinks of why she should remember, she'll write the reason down on a piece of paper and keep the paper in her change-purse all the time.

She has thought about giving up Griffin in spite of
their shared memory, though. Slowly, his face is losing its
sharpness — his sketchy letters, infrequent and short
phone calls are not enough to keep the home fires burning
strongly enough, faithfully enough. Oh yes, she entertains
the idea, especially when she re-reads his last postcard:

WEATHER HERE IS FABULOUS, FABULOUS VEGETARIAN
SHOPS, DRESSED UP LIKE A WOMAN FOR THIS
CARNIVAL IN KÖLN AND MET SOME FABULOUS
PEOPLE. THAT'S ME, THE CROSS-DRESSER! HAVING
A FABULOUS TIME. JUST FINISHED READING A
REALLY FABULOUS BOOK. CAN'T REMEMBER THE
TITLE, BUT IT'S FABULOUS. YOU HAVE TO READ IT.
CHANGED MY ARRIVAL DEPARTURE DATE TO A
BIT LATER. DON'T WAIT UP! HO HA HA.
FABULOUS. AUF WIEDERSEHEN, GRIFFIN!!

Carmen cuts the postcard up into tiny square pieces
and scatters the fragments in the back alley behind her
parents' house.

Kevin dances for Carmen.

You know why? he asks.

No. Why?

Because your name means "song." In Latin, I mean.

And Kevin swivels his hips in time to the music of her name. Carmen drives home at one o'clock in the morning. Can't read the street signs because her eyes are so blurry from tears when she thinks about Griffin obviously going crazy all by himself in Europe. What is Köln? Is that the same as Cologne? Why is he speaking German all of a sudden? He can barely say "kindergarten" correctly.

"Auf Wiedersehen" her little round brown ass! Give that bugger Griffin the finger is all she wants to do, but still she cries a little more. She can tell when she's being dumped.

She pulls into an all-night drugstore to buy more condoms. Kevin always buys the kind that make her itch. It's all Griffin's fault. He pushed her into Kevin's arms. She may not be loyal to Griffin with her body, but even though he doesn't deserve it, he always has her *mind.*

Kevin's Aunty Demeter hunched over the kitchen table with Kevin's mum, the air thick with cigarette smoke, Demeter's voice raspy and sharp from too many cigarettes. Arranging her autumn wedding, Demeter caws and cackles over bridal magazines, fusses over fabric colours and crepe paper, samples bits of wedding cake between gulps of homemade strawberry margarita, the two women's favourite drink. Aunt Dee with her long red fingernails giving Kevin the gold paper from her cigarette packages, her eyes narrowed from the smoke curling up from her cigarette and forming a wreath around her head.

I want Kevin to be my ring-bearer, says Dee. Here's his outfit. Aunt Dee pushes a sketch across the table littered with candied almonds and cigarette ash at Kevin's mum who picks up the sketch with both hands and peers at the tiny letters. Mother of pearl buttons, she reads. This is not going to be cheap. You sure you can't cut down on some of the frills? You sure you need mother of pearl buttons, fake pearl buttons will do the same job. And Kevin's not the cleanest kid, he'll dirty up a white velvet suit before he's even put on his underwear.

The happiest day of my life and already you're trying to ruin things, says Aunt Dee.

Kevin's mum lowers her eyes. Snorts.

I want Kevin to lead your dog Pepe down the aisle. This is a new thing I've heard about, having dog attendants. We'll decorate Pepe with purple chrysanthemums to match my bouquet and tie ribbons all along his back, you know like those horses on the merry-go-round from when we were kids. You know the merry-go-round I'm talking about? We'll give Pepe a purple ribbon for a leash and Kevin can walk with him up the aisle ahead of me. Also I hear in Korea ducks are part of the wedding procession because they mate for life. I wonder where I could get my hands on some ducks?

Kevin's mum nods, stubs out her cigarette. Coughs.

I swear, says his mum the next day, if she weren't my sister, I would've killed her by now. Stone cold dead. Yikes, watch it, here she comes! Wonder what in the hell she wants now. Kevin's mum runs to the front door, plasters a smile on her face.

Aunty Dee swirls into the house carrying bags of sample plastic ducks and more strawberries and tequila.

What was that phone call? demands Demeter. What was that lousy phone message I found saying you didn't think chocolate cake is appropriate? What was that?

Good to see you too Dee, says Kevin's mum. Let me help carry some of those bags into the kitchen.

Don't pull this good to see you Dee crap. I'm not that slow. I know when you think my ideas are stupid.

All I'm saying is maybe you better stick to fruit cake. That's what people use for weddings. That's what it says in the books.

Milo and I want chocolate! shouts Demeter. Her voice is so loud Kevin can hear her on the other side of the house.

Chocolate cake! Demeter yells. Milo's favourite flavour is chocolate, you know that, and I'm having a hard enough time getting him involved in all this. So when he says chocolate cake, then we have chocolate cake.

But fruit cake is traditional.

Fruit cake should be used for door stoppers, fruit cake is for fairies and visits to the old folks' home. In addition to which it tastes like hell! You know I hate fruit cake, how could you think of such a thing as fruit cake for my wedding?

But chocolate cake isn't firm enough, only fruit cake will hold all the layers and pillars you wanna load this cake down with, chocolate just isn't going to cut it. Trust me.

66

Trust you? How can I trust you, Ruby, when you won't listen to a word I'm saying?

Dee, I've been baking cakes since I was a teenager, I have baked your birthday cake every year since you learned how to talk. I guess I know what is or isn't going to work, and what is or isn't traditional. Chocolate cake is not going to work unless you have a smaller-sized cake.

The size stays.

Fine. You bake the cake. I quit.

How can I enjoy the happiest day of my life when I know I'm going to have to gag down a big log of fruit cake at the end of it? You know I have a delicate digestive system! You're just jealous, you're just jealous that I'm having a big wedding and that you didn't get one.

Aunty Dee, says Kevin, can I have your gold paper? Aunty Dee sniffles pathetically into a handful of paper doilies. All I want, she whispers, is to have the happiest day of my life be the happiest day of my life.

Aunty Dee used to play badminton with Kevin and Pepe in the back yard, play fetch with Pepe who was cute but not smart enough to remember that fetch didn't mean to eat the stick. Before she got engaged, Aunty Demeter was the best aunt in the world.

Dee, calm down, says Kevin's mother, her hand on Demeter's shoulder. You'll ruin your complexion for the wedding. Just calm yourself. I will bake you a beautiful chocolate cake, I will do my best to stop the cake from imploding from all the layers. All I'm saying is that you're going to have to expect a smaller cake. Oh my God, Demeter? Kevin's mum pulls back her hand. Demeter? Oh my God, your face, your face — you're . . . you're . . . you're turning into an asshole!

Demeter whirls her face to the nearest mirror. Kevin's mum is right. Dee's warm and lovely round face is now pink as Pepe's little anus, her features squinched up until they have disappeared, the skin gathered and folded in tightly around her hole of a mouth which has drifted up to the middle of her face.

Demeter screams, runs to the bathroom and locks the door.

Call Milo, Demeter screeches. Tell him the wedding is off, tell him I'm terminally ill and can never see him again, tell him, tell him — .

Don't be ridiculous Dee, says Kevin's mum. The money has already been spent, cancelling the wedding would be foolhardy. We'll figure something out.

Kevin's mum sits at her sewing machine for days and on the third day lifts up the thickest, longest, most luscious veil in the universe.

See, says Kevin's mum, prettier than your old face even.

It's beautiful, whimpers Demeter. It's the most beautiful veil I've ever seen. Dee starts to cry. Smothers Kevin's mum in a sad bear hug.

Kevin's mum says Dee has to keep her face covered for the entire wedding, no bones about it. Dee tells Milo that her skin's broken out in a terrible rash and could they please forget about lifting up her veil to kiss at the end of the ceremony? Of course she loves him, but she can't see him right now, she's too embarrassed. They'll spend the rest of their lives together after the wedding, it's just that now it would be better if she were alone. Separation will make their love fresh for the wedding.

At the wedding dinner, Aunt Dee sits at the head table, not touching her food, she can't open her mouth that wide. Her lips won't allow anything thicker than a straw or a cigarette past them, and she no longer has teeth. She sits and drinks ladylike alcoholic drinks through a straw poked up under her veil. The more she sucks the sweet strawberry-flavoured tequila, the more relaxed she feels. She made it through the day. Lasting out the day is what counted and it wasn't the biggest disaster of her life, no, it went quite smoothly, considering. She orders a mai tai and perches the umbrella in her tiara before downing the drink in several strong, swift sucks at her straw. What was she worried about? The cake is lovely, her dress is lovely, no one can see her face. Pepe and Kevin with the ring pillow were lovely, everything is lovely. Lovely lovely lovely.

The happiest day of her life.

The band starts to play and she slings her train over her shoulder, grabs a piña colada. She and Milo waltz to the first song together, her veil a screen between them. She invites Ruby and Kevin up to dance, they all dance together holding hands in a circle, the four of them, and sing along.

Thanks, she whispers in Kevin's mum's ear and for the first time since the engagement smiles as much as her face will let her.

Demeter drinks more, dances more, smiles more. She chats tipsily with the guests, pinches Milo's bum.

Hey big boy, she whispers in his ear, let's dance.

They dance closely, her sweat seeps large visible stains into the fabric of her dress under the arms. Demeter realizes she's boiling to death and without thinking raises her veil.

Milo stops dancing.

You said you had a rash, says Milo. What rash? I don't see no rash! I didn't get to see you for three months because of a horrible rash and it turns out you don't have a rash at all?

You mean that?

Yeah I mean that. Maybe you're a little sweaty but I can take care of that.

Milo pulls a hanky from his jacket pocket, cups her face and wipes her forehead gently. He smiles.

He lights her a cigarette and they do the bird-dance in the middle of the ballroom floor, strut around like chickens in time to the music and give each other drunken sloppy kisses like any other newly married couple. The happiest day of their lives.

When Griffin's plane arrives, he takes a cab to his mother's house, dumps his backpack, phones his friends. They arrange to play pool at Kevin's. Maybe drink a beer or two. He has much to tell them, after a while he just stopped writing anyone, too much of a bother to write, he was too busy living. He'll do some joe-job for a while, save his money, live at his mum's a little longer, then take off for Thailand. Sinks the three into the corner pocket. Sucks loudly at the cold sharp bubbles of beer.

Anyone wanna Camel? he asks, and offers the opened cigarette package all around. He pops one in his mouth.

Wish I could quit, he says. Smoking's a disgusting habit, and he grins like an emaciated Marlboro man.

Two days pass before Carmen phones him, asks, What's going on? How long you been in town? You were in town two days and you didn't phone me? You didn't bother to let me know you were here?

Maybe you don't understand, he says, I thought I explained it in my postcard.

You explained what in your postcard? What postcard? she says, and she cries for three days straight, the top of her head lopped off from her broken heart. She phones Kevin, leftover crying snot still blocking her sinuses, and fucks him until his eyeballs roll back into his head and stay there. Carmen. His favourite song.

So what if I'm Griffin's friend? thinks Kevin. It's only because we've known each other since elementary school. Friends since we were practically babies, but not necessarily *friendly*. Fair's fair, Griffin buggers off and Carmen is left alone. Kevin has no choice. It's not Kevin's *fault*.

After, Kevin prepares Carmen a bowl of instant potato soup.

Haven't had time to do groceries, he says. Sorry. He strokes her hair as she cries into her soup, he watches her tears and bubbles of snot plop into the creamed potato surface.

Carmen learns that there is never satisfaction in playing Penelope to some prick's Ulysses.

Now that Griffin has abandoned her, Carmen tries to run into him.

Every morning she is meticulous with her appearance. He always liked her hair up with ringlets, so she puts it up and uses a curling iron on her hair. Ringlets love her black hair so she gives her hair more and more ringlets, a ringlet explosion. Not like the old white days. He liked her in short skirts — she wears skirts so short she can hardly breathe without exposing herself.

She drinks coffee at his favourite coffee shop.

Sees movies at his favourite movie theatre.

She attends events that would appeal to him, Star Trek conventions, poetry readings.

Over the course of months she meets too many people who advise her how she could do her hair to look more like Lieutenant Uhura, hears too many poems by people who couldn't string a coherent sentence together if their lives depended on it, and gets shaky from caffeine, but Griffin never appears. He must be avoiding her.

She shops in natural food stores, the more hardcore vegetarian the better because Fran makes Griffin eat meat in her house no matter how much he protests, so naturally he'll have to find a way to clean all that animal blood from his body. Carmen browses through the shelves, runs her fingers over bins of lentils, soybeans, garbanzo, pinto, black turtle, adzuki and lima beans. The air in the shop smells of unpolished wood, heavy spices. She saunters through the oil aisle. Oil aisle oil aisle, she whispers to herself; her boots clump on the floor, she unties her scarf from around her neck and drapes it over her shoulders. Corn oil, canola, safflower, almond, peanut. She stops, peers over the shelf and scans the store for any sign of her errant Griffin. Monosaff, avocado, olive oil. Olive oil. She understands olive oil, nothing too exotic or fruit-loopy about olive oil and she picks up the bottle, then puts it down immediately when she sees the price. Ridiculous. She takes off her coat, straightens her short skirt, slings her coat over her arm.

Heads over to the next aisle, keeping an eye out for any six-foot-four, broomstick-shaped men. Engevita yeast, brewer's yeast, yeast flakes. Bacon-flavoured tofu strips, chicken-flavoured tofu nuggets, organic lettuce, beets, apples.

Tea.

She can relate to tea. Boxes and boxes of tea. How organic can tea get? Menstrual, fasting, calming, laxative, PMS, bedtime, woman's cycle, echinacea plus, chamomile, spearmint, peppermint, peppermint-spearmint teas.

Choosing the right tea takes a lot of good browsing time, a lot of looking-around-for-Griffin time. She can spend up to a good one and a half hours selecting the right tea in a single store.

She gives herself one and a half months, then asks Griffin to a movie. Griffin there? she asks. Phoning is so simple, she wonders why she didn't think of it before.

One moment please, says Fran, poor old fucked up Fraaan. Obviously pretending not to recognize Carmen's voice.

Of course Griffin agrees to go out with her. How could he not?

She changes her blouse four times, decides on baggy but clean jeans, doesn't want him to think she dressed up for him or anything. She lotions her skin twice, her skin so dry in the winter, but also because she loves the way it looks. Loves the way it glistens, moves so warm. Her hair pours with ringlets.

They see *The Ten Commandments* at the rep theatre. He asks her afterward if she wants to go for coffee? Does she need a ride home?

Sure, she says, his body familiar in her arms, and he hasn't had sex in a long time, not since he left Europe. Maybe just this once and then never again. He wants to stay faithful to Renata.

Renata would understand.

Carmen goes to university for one more year, then gets a job as a gofer at a small insurance company. No chance of upward movement, but at last she has money, and she pays off student loans, VISA bills, has a travel fund for a trip, maybe to the hot springs next year. She moves into her own apartment, a shitty little basement suite with new carpeting that makes her eyes and nose run, but at least she has her own *space*. Now she and Griffin can have sex wherever and whenever they want. Not that they do. Too tired from working all day. When they have enough money saved up, Carmen and Griffin will travel. No way in hell is he going to Thailand, she tells him, the West Coast is the farthest away he'd better plan. Griffin landscapes full time, all the time. Seen too much of life to want to go back to school. She makes more than he does and she's secretly proud of this.

At Carmen's new job, Ruth the receptionist bakes cookies and cupcakes for the office every Monday. Ruth's designated herself the Monday morning cookie patrol.

Need a little something to get into gear, being Monday and all, says Ruth, as she bites into a shortbread cookie. Have one, Ruth says, Take two.

Carmen's the newest employee. The first month passes along fine, just fine. The other employees are stressed and unfriendly so she keeps herself company, pretends not to notice when they go for lunches and don't invite her along. All part of being the new kid on the block, the rookie, the stranger.

Ruth sits on the edge of Carmen's desk, a plate of cupcakes sprinkled with little silver balls in her hand. Carmen's most important papers squinched up under Ruth's bum.

So this guy phoned in Friday because he got in an accident and his car insurance account was in arrears, says Ruth. You want me to leave? I can leave and let you get on with your work if you want.

Ruth holds out the plate. Carmen takes the smallest cupcake, bites into it, the icing globs in the corners of her lips. One of the silver balls falls off her cupcake into her lap, rolls between her legs.

No. I'm not busy, says Carmen. Carmen's the newest employee. She doesn't want to alienate anyone.

Then have another cupcake. For the road. Anyway, so this man phones in Friday and I say to him, now sir, you're covered but I notice you're in arrears on last month's bill. Had one of those Indian names, with Smiling Bear or Howling Wolf or whatever in it. Not to sound racist or anything, says Ruth, but Natives never pay their bills on time. Welcome to the twentieth century, kemo sabay. I put him through this time, but next time I'm not gonna be so soft.

Really, says Carmen. Really Carmen should say something. Next time she'll say something.

The next week is lemon tarts.

You like lemons? asks Ruth. Full of vitamin C. Have I shown you a picture of my nephew? Here he is, says Ruth. She thrusts a small brass-framed photo at Carmen.

He's six. Sweet, eh? I know everyone says this about their kids but he is *really* smart for his age. He can already count to one hundred! He's a genius! Especially compared to the other kids in his class, his mother was telling me. I've always heard that Chinese people are smarter, his class is full of them, but he's at the top, the very top of the class. So much for that.

Now Carmen will say something. She flounders in her head for something to say.

Have another tart? asks Ruth.

No. No thanks. I don't really care for tarts.

There, Carmen said something.

Yeah, I made the crust maybe a little too thick this time.

Mostly Carmen tries not to hear Ruth, tries not to think of how Rama and Kevin would react to Ruth's lemon tart bullshit. They wouldn't put up with any of it. Carmen's not that strong, she just absorbs the words with her skin, lets them eat into the lining of her stomach. Ruth isn't very smart anyway, she consoles herself. Ruth's French braid is untidy. Ruth has bad breath. Ruth will burn in hell.

So why don't you just say something? says Griffin. What's so hard about just telling her to fuck off? Just say to her, look Ruth, f-u-c-k o-f-f. It's that simple. You want me to go in and do it for you?

Carmen makes her plan of attack. Next time, next time she will tell Ruth what's on her mind. Tell Ruth to stop it.

You going to the Stampede this year? asks Ruth.

No, says Carmen. Carmen's body stiffens, she bares her teeth, her hackles rise. Now Carmen will tell Ruth. How will she say it? "Ruth, you can't say those things," she'll say. Or, "That's offensive. Please stop making those sorts of remarks." Or, best of all, "Ruth, that's totally racist," she'll say jokingly and pat Ruth on the back.

No, me neither, says Ruth. Too many rednecks.

Cherry cheesecake tart week.

My car wouldn't start yesterday, says Ruth, and I had to call a cab, I just hate calling a cab in this city, always driven by some Sikh or Sheik or whatever you call 'em in the turbans and the upholstery just reeks of curry, gets in your clothes and on your skin worse than cigarette smoke. As soon as I got in the door home, I threw my clothes in the washing machine and jumped in the shower.

Carmen blurts her coffee back into her cup, spits out at Ruth, What do you call me behind my back? Sammy Davis Jr.? Can I do a little soft shoe for ya?

Carmen is aghast, she sits rooted at her desk for the entire day, doesn't leave for lunch, for coffee break, not even to go to the toilet. She pretends to work and work, but plays the scene over and over again in her head. Sammy Davis Jr. Brilliant.

Ruth loudly offers food and chats to all the other employees, but only sticks her head in Carmen's office doorway.

Cupcake? Ruth asks.

Okay, says Carmen, embarrassed.

Ruth sets a cupcake on a paper towel on the edge of Carmen's desk, then quickly backs out of the office.

Carmen works at her desk, goes for coffee, eats her lunch alone. Ruth quits to have a baby. Everyone in the office throws Ruth a half-hearted baby shower and Carmen even buys Ruth a card in addition to putting in money for the car-seat from everyone in the office. "Break a leg Ruth," says the card.

The morning after Ruth's goodbye party, Carmen walks into the office building as usual, nods at herself in the mirrored wall leading up to the office. Excellent, she thinks. Ringlet party on her head, Midnight Madness on her mouth. Carmen walks past the reception desk, does a double take.

You're the new receptionist? asks Carmen.

Yes.

What's your name?

Mika.

Where do you come from, Japan?

Fuck off.

Excellent. Can I get you a coffee? A leftover cupcake or a shortbread cookie?

Maybe a cookie, says Mika.

Sorry I said that. I've been working here too long.

Carmen invites Mika out for coffee every day. Hounds Mika to go out for lunch.

Carmen complains to Mika about work, warns her about the food in the cafeteria, the coffee in the dispenser in the hallway. Carmen scrabbles with her nails and clings to Mika like a drowning rat. One evening Griffin comes to pick Carmen up from work, gives Mika the eye.

This is my friend Mika, Griffin. Mika, this is my fiancé Griffin. Just let me get my gear packed up in the office, says Carmen, and she skips off. A new friend. A precious husband-to-be.

Never slept with an Asian woman before, Griffin thinks. Hi, he says.

Tell your beau I'm a lesbian, says Mika.

What? asks Carmen. What? She comes out of her tiny office, papers in her hands. A what? What the hell's going on? She stabs Griffin in the cheek with a sharp fingernail when they get to the car. They don't speak to each other for three days.

Carmen is disappointed that her ideal friendship with Mika has to be complicated by homosexuality. Now Carmen has to wonder if maybe Mika's been watching her in a sexual way and this is the reason Mika's been so nice and easy to get along with. In theory, Mika being a lesbian doesn't bother Carmen, but Carmen goes out of her way to hide her breasts under heavy sweaters, and wears long baggy pants. Mika doesn't look or act like any lesbian she's ever seen on talk shows on TV. Carmen watches Mika for lesbian signs like armpit or leg hair. Carmen once did see Mika wearing a black leather jacket and walking a white toy poodle. Motorcycle jacket — isn't that part of the uniform? Mika also has four earrings in one ear and only one earring in the other ear. Perhaps the earrings are some kind of code.

So what are you up to tonight? asks Mika.

Carmen wonders if this is some kind of lesbian come-on. Her hands start to shake. What can Carmen say without hurting Mika's feelings, yet clearly show she's hetero-sexual? She's not prepared to become a lesbian. She's finally gotten her life together. What could two women do together anyway? It would be boring. Too many breasts.

Oh. Griffin and I are just staying home, or no, I mean we're going out to a movie. With friends. A married couple we know.

That's nice.

Two months later Mika hands in her resignation.

I found a better-paying job, Mika says. Not much upward mobility, but the environment is good. It's been a real pleasure working here.

Really Mika means that the fucking insurance office is full of fucking idiots. The office, in fact, is so right-wing Mika wants to puke. Right-wing freaks! rants Mika to her sister over and over again. No one human could stand it! Mika and Carmen drink white wine over a goodbye lunch, get a little tipsy and giggle over how great it would be if the boss died. Just keeled over one day plop from clogged arteries or some unidentified, non-contagious virus. They know he will never die, never retire, he refuses to even acknowledge illness — comes to work with bronchitis and within the week someone catches it.

The boss spreads his germs like he signs their paycheques twice a month — with oozing power.

Carmen and Mika subside into tipsy silence. Stare at the tablecloth.

So, are you seeing anyone? A little clumsily Carmen thinks, because she doesn't know if lesbians actually "see" each other. Maybe there's another word.

No. I'm taking a rest, says Mika.

Really what Carmen wants to know is what women actually do together, but she drinks her wine instead and dribbles it on the front of her blouse.

They finish lunch, polish off the bottle of wine and run, tipsy and giggling, to the corner store for breath mints.

I wish you didn't have to go, says Carmen. I'll miss you.

What she really means is that once again she'll be the only person of colour in the office. Forced to stand alone, make decisions as to whether or not telling someone to fuck off is worth the trouble.

Well there's always the phone, says Mika. She pushes the mint into her cheek.

What Mika really means is she doesn't, never did, and never will expect Carmen to be her friend. Carmen has too many hang-ups, cares more about her hair than what really matters. She is so obviously confused, confused and awkward about a lot of things, including her own body. She acts like she comes from Pluto. Why doesn't Carmen just let her hair down out of all those elastics and barrettes and Shirley Temple ringlets and be done with it?

Yeah, says Carmen. That's true.

They hug goodbye, but only so that the fronts of their coats touch. A nipple-brushing A-shaped hug. Carmen loses Mika's number in the front pocket of one of her blazers.

Carmen and Griffin are not invited for Sunday dinners at Fran's house. Fran doesn't even want them in the same city. Fran confronts Griffin while he packs his clothes into boxes, blocks the way to his closet with her body, spit flying from her mouth, caking in the corners of her lips; her chest heaves irregularly, watch her, she's going to have a heart attack, she'll have a stroke and then what will he do, she's the only mother he'll ever have, isn't that just like men, leaving always leaving just when you need them the most. How could he do this, go off with that *dog*, doesn't he know about AIDS, what sluts black women are? Just don't go and get married because no matter what the law says she'll never see any marriage between them as legal, and don't ever ever have kids, they'll only be bastards, they won't be any grandchildren of *hers*, little *nigger* babies.

Griffin accepts Fran's reaction as part of menopause. Carmen smashes her brand new glass coffee table with a marble vase full of brown-eyed susans when Griffin tells her what Fran said. Godfrey books another research expedition, this time to the Arctic for the entire winter. He realizes Fran will need the entire house to herself in order to crawl the walls unimpeded. And that little pencil-holder of a man she sleeps with, well, as long as he keeps Fran busy. The New Boss doesn't seem to do much else, he's screwing Fran pretty much continuously — his business must run itself by magic. God knows.

Fran goes to work as usual, visits the New Boss more than usual, but all she can do is sit in the chair across from his desk. Stare at her reflection in the lenses of his horn-rimmed glasses. He can give her nothing she wants. She has a bitter burning hole in her heart, pepper sprinkled into a fire. If Carmen and Griffin get married, Fran will die. She will shrivel up and die.

Now that she is older, now that she realizes its purpose, Carmen understands the importance of marriage. Griffin is impossible to pin down otherwise; if she'd married him *before* he left for Europe, even though it was financially impossible, they could have avoided his temporary insanity and disorientation, and her infidelity with Kevin.

She explains to Kevin that, although she finds him intensely attractive, Griffin is the man she is going to marry, she and Griffin are meant to ruffle their feathers together and will eventually settle down to building their lifelong nest. Finally have those cocoa babies.

Well there's always Sadie, says Kevin. She's no chopped liver, you know.

Carmen's left eyebrow arches as she reconsiders the existence of Sadie.

Yes. Well. Sadie. Of course. Sadie's a lucky girl.

Of course Carmen is jealous of Sadie. She gives Kevin a long goodbye kiss, they squiggle their tongues in each other's mouths. This is a good trick.

Being married to Griffin, she will have the law and everyone else on her side, maybe even Fraaan's final defeat, and Griffin will be obliged to love her forever.

Marriage is an institution she has developed infinite respect for, an organization, she feels, she will gladly enter in her white or more likely off-white gown, veil and cascade of flowers, slamming the door behind her, loudly proudly. Marriage solves problems, commands respect and approval. That oh so subtle nod of the waiter's head as he notices their matching gold rings, her hyphenated name on the list of reservations, the waiter leading them to their table in an expensive restaurant. What a lovely young couple, people at the other tables will say, whereas now Carmen and Griffin are hardly ever noticed except as an odd, interracial couple. Just lovers. Illicit, slumming with a member of another race before really settling down. Or worse, people probably think she's his mistress, while his real white wife waits at home.

At their wedding they will be showered with gifts and money. She and Griffin will have life insurance policies, tax benefits, joint bank accounts, RRSPs, car payments on a family-sized minivan or four-by-four. Their love for each other cemented by the rings on the third finger of their left hands. They will play bridge with another married couple like Carmen's parents did when she was young — the achingly lovely symmetry of two married couples playing a card game requiring four players, two teams. A bridge team. If they try to divorce, God forbid, there will be alimony, marriage counselling and they will probably stay together anyway for the sake of the kids. *Marriage* counselling. No such thing as "*lover* counselling," no such thing as "*common-law* counselling." Marriage guarantees.

At other people's weddings she elbows her way grimly to the front of the crowd of single women and snaps the thrown bouquet from the air like a frog traps a wing-spread beetle. With automaton regularity she clinks and bangs her forks, spoons, knives against her wine glass, water glass, gin and tonic glass, any vessel that rings, and doesn't stop until the wedding couple kiss their mouths raw and the dinner settings are taken away.

With her coaching, Griffin is almost as good as Carmen at catching brides' garters. No mercy, says Carmen and his body becomes perfectly horizontal as he dives for the garter and slides to a stop, his head centimetres away from the podium. At his cousin's wedding he sprains his ankle, accuses the best man of getting in his way; but Griffin catches the garter anyway, stretches it into a tight headband around his forehead and poses for numerous photos.

Carmen inspects all the garters, throw-away polyester or real satin, ribbons and lace or just ribbon. She examines her bouquets to the tiniest leaf, and adds to her list what flowers her own bouquet will have, whether or not to include ivy, whether or not her garter will be satin or silk or polyester. Griffin drapes the garters over the rear-view mirror of his secondhand truck.

She compares wedding themes. Winter wonderland? Cotton Club in the roaring twenties? Caribbean island? Or maybe a Hallowe'en theme? She could dress up as the bride of Frankenstein and Griffin could be the Wolfman. She watches vows being exchanged, rewrites and revises her own vows in her head. So far, she has her wedding planned down to the tiny packages of groom's cake wrapped in silver paper and lace ribbon placed at every guest's place setting. Of course the groom's cake flower decoration will vary depending on what theme she finally chooses.

This time she won't let him slip away — forget about giving him space, obviously he doesn't know how to handle it. Too much space and he'll end up on the moon.

She has saved one thousand, two hundred and thirty-four dollars.

She decides that they will get married in a year. By then they will have enough money. She tells Griffin to get a practice hair cut, and registers them in a ballroom dancing course so they won't look like oafs on the wedding dance floor.

Carmen sits in the high swivel chair at the black hair salon and stares in the mirror while Dr. J runs his fingers over her scalp, upward through her hair. Her hair stands up in rays around her face, the sun.

This ringlet deal has got to go, he says.

But ringlets will look perfect with the tiara I'm getting.

By the time you *get* your tiara you won't have any hair left! You're burning all your hair off with that curling iron.

Well what then?

Cut them off. You've got a nice shaped head. Cut your hair short. We'll deep condition your head, get the frizz out. You won't look so much like that dumb-ass Shirley Temple. You've got a pretty face, why do you want to hide it behind all these dumb-ass, high maintenance springs?

And because her hairdresser Dr. J is her guru, she agrees, even though he hurt her feelings with the Shirley Temple remark.

When she gets home from the hair salon she jumps under the bed covers and cries so hard her eyes swell up to escargot shells. She'll look a fool in her veil and tiara with hair like this! Her old white hair is what she wants, she's been kidding herself all along. A nice long, coiled French braid, or a smooth, loopy chignon, her bangs sprayed and sparkling high up on her forehead, droopy ringlets at the sides of her head that sag and fall out at the end of the day. The hair curls tightly against her head, she tentatively feels the warm shape of her skull under her new tight hair with her hands. Griffin brings her pizza in bed. Love your funky do baby, he says. Flicks on the TV.

She stares at the inside of the bedspread, TV light shining through. I think the wedding colours should be silver and pink, she says.

She wears large shiny metal earrings because her head, she's found, is so so little without its hair. Low maintenance hair. This is after all what she likes. Although straight hair, from when she was white, was nice too. Not *as* nice, not *as* low maintenance. French braids — who was she trying to kid? She smears on another coat of Midnight Madness. Consults Dr. J about what eyeshadow won't clash with her wedding pearls. She could wear a veil if it were fastened on with flowers.

Griffin phones his mother.

Ma, he says, we've decided to get married this summer.

Silence.

Ma?

I can't hear you, Fran says. I didn't hear what you just said. Sorry, I don't know what you're talking about. What did you say? This is obviously an obscene phone call! Get off my phone!

Fran's fingers, then her left arm go dead, her head goes dead. She drools on the kitchen linoleum where she has fallen, her poodle hairdo squashed on the side from lying on the floor so long. She was chopping onions when Griffin called, had her seizure in mid-chop, chopped off the tip of her left index finger, then fell to the floor.

Ma, says Griffin. Ma? he asks. Carmen stands off to the side of the hospital bed rolling her eyes, horribly glad.

Please don't get married please don't get married please don't get married please don't get married please don't get married. These are the only words Fran can say. Fran drags her hands up in prayer. Her hands, they notice, are covered in a red, pimply rash. Carmen wants to shove her, bed and all, out the window.

I can't do it, says Griffin. I can't marry you with my mother like this. He pulls Carmen's engagement ring off her finger, sets it on his bedside table.

I bought the ring, says Carmen. If you would be so kind as to give it back to its owner.

Carmen wants to scream, wants to grab Griffin, one hand on each of his ears and smash their foreheads together. She grabs the ring, shoves it onto her hand where it belongs.

It's killing her, he says. Maybe we should wait.

Wait for what? Wait for her to stop being a frothing racist? Wait for her to get her head out of her curdled milk-white ass? Let her die, says Carmen, I won't miss her. I'm not going to let her ruin my life. She's manipulating you Griffin, she's manipulating us. Can't you see that? Can't you get that through your thick, fat skull? She's trying to sabotage our lives!

Carmen sees she's gone too far. In his head, Griffin leaves her forever. Fran has put her foot down. Carmen should have known it would end when Fran finally put down her foot, a hiking boot squarely on top of a sprawling daddy-long-legs. Carmen's six legs bend and snap, her curly black head crushed to a smear.

Carmen has long intimate conversations with Griffin's answering machine:

Griffin, are you sure about this, Griffin, think about it, I'm *really sorry* about what I said, Griffin? Griffin? It was just the shock, I didn't know what I was saying, I love you Griffin, I want to *marry* you, we belong together, Griffin? Please answer the phone. Goddammit Griffin, I've already booked the hall and bought my dress! The invitations have been SENT!

She dumps the wedding dress, elbow length veil, satin pumps *and* the silver groom's cake paper in the garbage. Her wedding day, her Griffin, her cocoa babies, she buries in the mourning black of Glad garbage bags, this is the best day of her life. She vomits in celebration, vomits on the dress, stomach acid rising up, a tidal wave, behind her nose. She is now a dark plastic angel.

Crows pick among the white satin garbage. She gulps from the bottle of Maalox. Maalox keeps down the gnaw of her new ulcer, the small coiled ball nestled between her ribs. At their apartment, Carmen pretends to blend herself in with the shadows. Wears only black clothes, switches to drinking tiny cups of black coffee, no milk, no sugar, nothing but Maalox immediately after her morning cup. Buys only dried mourning flowers for the vases in the apartment.

Griffin dumped me, Rachel, says Carmen. Carmen bites into a chocolate bar. Puts the money down on the counter in front of Rachel.

Try this, says Rachel. Rachel unwraps a tube of lipstick and rubs some of the lipstick on the back of Carmen's hand.

It's an ultra-dark colour. Called Mocha Panther. Good name, eh?

At work the Friday before her wedding day, Carmen accidentally knocks her head loudly on the book shelf next to the boss's office door on the top floor, and her stomach gives a spasm that tears her Mocha Panther lips off. But the only sound that comes from the office is the hopeless buzz of a fly bumping the window.

Carmen gets home Friday afternoon, picks up the remote control, settles into the black plastic casing of the television set and disappears.

Fran lies in bed, her hands locked in prayer. The red rash, now turned purple, consumes her entire body. Fran's health is sand dunes — unreliable, dry and gritty. The stroke has left her brain untouched, but taken away many parts of her purpled body; she can do nothing but think. She thinks the hospital smells too much like urine. Obviously someone in housekeeping isn't doing her job. She is repulsed by the sight of the bed-pan she must use, humiliated at having her bum wiped, a grown woman, not even that sick. Having to be fed, washed, watered; helpless and subject to Griffin's reading whims.

Griffin reads aloud to her from *Gardener's Monthly*.

How to grow beautiful kale, he reads, and then he settles back in his chair with a smile on his face and reads aloud to her from articles on growing herb window boxes, fertilizing spider plants, getting your cactus to bloom.

Griffin leaves giant orange chrysanthemums on her bedside table, on her window sill. She *hates* orange. The only thing she doesn't mind is the New Boss's visits. He picks peonies from his wife's garden and centres them on the bedside table. Sometimes, through the hospital's dense urine-antiseptic smell, she can breathe wafts of the peonies' freshness.

God sends her a Get Well card, says he can't get away just yet, but will be with her as soon as possible. She plucks at the covers. Irritated. Get Well card her sweet pitoot. The New Boss bought her an expensive and oh so sexy bed jacket in *addition* to a subscription to *Maclean's,* her all-time favourite magazine.

She remembers the last time she saw her mother, also using a bedpan, just before Griffin was born. Her mother Bedelia was confined before her death, but in a nursing home. Bedelia, out of her mind as usual, her nightgown falling away and exposing her breasts. The practical nurse helps Fran give Bedelia a sponge bath, shows her where the pan is stored if Bedelia needs it.

Mornings when Bedelia sings, says the nurse, she's the rival of the most talented canary.

The hooks and eyes on Bedelia's gown bite into her flesh, squalling with a violent pimply rash. The nurse, puzzled, rubs ointment and moisturizers over the rash covering Fran's mother's body. Both women struggle with her as she trembles and strikes at her gown. The practical nurse and Bedelia's daughter are too young to understand that pin feathers need air to grow. Whoever heard of a bird with clothes?

Francie, Bedelia says.

Yes mother, says Fran.

There are two kinds of women in the world, Francie. The kind you marry and the kind you fuck.

Oh sweet Jesus, thinks Fran, only eighteen years old. She stands with her legs apart to gain balance, cups her left hand over her pregnant belly in readiness for the hair washing, her biweekly visit to her ancient mother. Her mother's ravings.

Two flats do not a note make. I'll fly like a bird. Just like mother, just like my mother's mother. My great-grandmother though, she didn't get to fly but turned into a fountain. Never told you that story did I? Probably because no one ever told me. I wonder how that happened. I get to be a bird though. Maybe when my wings are ready I'll fly and find her, get her to tell me. Get the story from the horse's mouth. I get to be a bird. I know it. Don't believe me Francie? Smell my breath. See? Bedelia pushes her face, skin soft as a nestling's, into Fran's and belches out a cloud of birdy air. Fran's mum rocks from Fran's pushing and pulling and cleaning of her old, bumpy and pimpled body. Fran is used to Bedelia's wild smells, used to the smooth hopelessness of the nursing home, of her mother's long since lost mind.

Two flats do not make a note. At the age of fourteen when Fran was a bridesmaid at her cousin's wedding, she kissed a distant female relative, Stephanie — kissed Stephanie on the lips not just because they were relatives but because Fran was in *love,* and Fran remembered the kiss for years. At the cousin's wedding she danced ballroom style with Stephanie, her hand on Stephanie's shoulder, then on her back.

Relax, says Stephanie, all of eighteen years old, and engaged even. Stephanie and Fran dance the tango they learned in gym class in different grades, trade male and female parts, Fran's warm palm on the bare and sweaty small of Stephanie's back where it fits most comfortably. Stephanie looks like she just stepped out of a movie, her breasts small and nearly invisible except for the tiny points of her nipples under her green silky sheath of a dress, Fran in white patterned cotton. They dance the tango, the fox trot, the polka. Stephanie hums sweetly until it's time to leave, the groomsmen and their gymnastic tricks have taken over the dance floor, and then Stephanie kisses Fran goodbye.

Goodbye, she says, and kisses Fran, surprised, on the lips — her lips not ready and her tongue hanging out a little, mushy and wet. Little Fran, her stomach round like a child's and her breasts only pop-eyed nipples; Stephanie so trim and female with her stylish bob and green silk. Stephanie with her fiancé Roy, his hand sliding covertly onto the smooth fabric covering her bum. Fran kisses Stephanie back, this time her tongue tucked in her mouth, Fran's lips pursed and red. A sweet, quick kiss to let Stephanie know Fran loves her. The fiancé smiles and draws Stephanie away. Dancers waltz and trip on the dance floor, the bride suffers through another dance with another old business friend of her father's, the groomsmen lift the groom up and bump his head through the hall ceiling, all the men clap and hoot.

Fran burns around the thought of Stephanie, so tall, slim and green. Her own body will never look like that, her breasts smooth decoration rather than an embarrassment. And a fiancé! Stephanie has gold threads in her hair, pure gold threads, Fran is certain. Even the small red pimple on Stephanie's chin is graceful, meaningful. Fran remembers her hand on Stephanie's naked back, Fran doesn't even mind the sweat, the smells of perfume, powder. Fran holds her palm to her nose, breathes on her skin to warm it up and revive the smells. She wants to be exactly like Stephanie some day, smell as good, be as much fun. Have a fiancé like Roy. Fran closes her eyes. Waltzes with herself.

Francie, asks Bedelia from the doorway, What are you doing?

I'm dancing, I'm dancing.

Head in the clouds, says Bedelia. You come on down to earth. My little accident. When we're dead we'll all be flying and dancing with the angels, maybe too much.

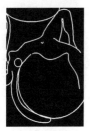

Fran spills her milk at dinner exactly a week after she dances with Stephanie at the wedding. Knocks it with a blind hand. The milk looks pretty splattered on the blue carpet. The white beads on the blue, the colours pretty and cool.

Francie! says Bedelia. She slaps the table with the palm of her hand so hard one of the peonies in the vase in the middle of the table tumbles out, spills petals and droplets of water on the polished wood.

Francie, stop that! Stop thinking! You keep those thoughts where they belong in the garbage with the rest of the trash. Two flats do not a note make, you hear me? You need a man because what are two women gonna do? I'll tell you what they're gonna do, they're gonna do nothing because no woman is natural without a man. No woman is natural! Francie! Trash!

Fran doesn't know what Bedelia is talking about. Fran sneaks a fallen petal, twists it between her fingers, twists and twists until the juice wets her fingers, seeps under her nails. She begins to cry. Warm, sea-salt tears she wipes away with her other hand, her sleeves, her skirt.

Peony blossoms the size of poodle heads, Fran's face wet and hot, heavy from the knotted and undecipherable bundle of words her mother has just placed on her head and shoulders. Peonies her favourite, peonies she picked and placed on the table, put her nose in every blossom before she cut the stem, used scissors from the kitchen drawer, sliced the flowers' heads off. She put her hand on Stephanie's back and kissed Stephanie goodbye on the lips. All the wedding guests saw, her mother saw, all the wedding guests thought, her mother *thought.* What?

No woman is natural. Fran is trash.

Stephanie certainly isn't trash, Fran being kissed by Stephanie, Fran kissing Stephanie, are not the actions or feelings of trash. But Fran has been named trash; trash blows through the streets, dogs nuzzle garbage cans for trash to eat. Fran drops the mulched peony petal from her hand. The petal falls in the bowl of her tear-spotted skirt. Falls again to her feet.

Francie!

Two flats do not a note make, says Bedelia. A phrase passed down from generation to generation so that it has barely any meaning, carries only a stench of confusion and panic. Fran grows so twisted with shame her gums slide away from her teeth and hairs, precious and irreplaceable, fall from her scalp. Her hairbrush thick with hair like a bird's nest. So she meets God because who else is there to meet? Her mother and their housekeeper push them together, long before Fran is ripe. He stakes his claim, becomes her boyfriend, holds her hand, kisses her chastely in the front doorway of her mother's house. Feels her breasts through her sweater after a year of dating, then succeeds in getting his hands up her shirt after two. Carries her books. That they will marry is inevitable.

When she is seventeen, she likes to wind embroidery thread around her wrist, watch the bloated colour of her hand shift from red to deep purple, the delicacy of slowly losing feeling, the ice of her fingertips on her legs, her cheeks, like a tongue poking an aching tooth again and again.

In the photographs of Fran and Godfrey's wedding, Fran smiles so hard the laminate on the photos has cracked. Almost all the photos have Bedelia positioned between the newlyweds, holding Fran by the elbow, her other hand firmly tucked into the crook of God's arm. The newlyweds fight on the day of the wedding, just before the ceremony.

Because of Fran having her menses, whispers Bedelia to relatives who care to know.

If any of these relatives had bothered to ask Fran, she would tell them that they fought because Godfrey told her she had no right to wear her wedding veil over her face. No right since she was barely a virgin, he knows. Even the white dress is inappropriate, he says.

It's bad luck to see the bride in her dress before the wedding, Fran snaps. Bugger off.

And Godfrey retreats, fuming, the cool and shameless skin of Fran's naked breasts still glowing on his palms.

God is full of shit of course, and Fran jams another hairpin into her headpiece. Full of *shit*. Her breasts are bound by the imprint of God's hands, the only part of her body she ever lets him touch. She is going to wear that veil over her face even if it makes her die of heat prostration. Let her be struck down by lightning for pretending to be purer than she is. She doesn't care.

She asks her maid of honour to sew the bottom edge of her veil to her bodice so that Godfrey can't lift the veil to kiss her but has to settle for her lips through the tulle. Titters from the wedding guests. Serve him right for being such a self-righteous pill. Bedelia allows them one photo alone together where they stand side by side, not looking at each other but staring straight ahead at the camera, and then she remains between them for the rest of the day, sturdy as a fencepost sunk in concrete.

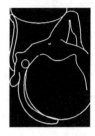

Bedelia in her nightgown gives a sudden squawk that Fran only half hears and believes comes from outside the window. That afternoon during nap time, the last day Fran sees her mother alive, Bedelia's rash bursts open and pin-feathers, then adult feathers, sprout through her pores. She stretches her wings and opens her sharp mouth wide, clicks it closed one two three times. This is how metamorphoses work; angry old women transform into magpies, white girls turn brown, lose their lovers, but discover themselves in the television set. Metamorphosis always signals a happy alternative.

Bedelia shits on the pillow, flies from the room. A farmer shoots at her but misses. Of course he misses. She's already dead.

What now? thinks Bedelia. What now? In her small skull she is no longer mother of Fran, or the daughter of

Fran's grandparents, but a hungry and cold brand new magpie, requiring nourishment and warmth. Her beak and wings slice through the air. She leans her bird-body west in the direction of British Columbia. West is where all heroes go when they retire. West to where she'll rest on the beach among rotting gull bodies and used hypodermics washed up on the sand. Maybe she'll look up her great-grandmother turned into a fountain, or her best friend Vesta who passed to the other side years ago. West is where heroes go.

Or this is what Fran would like to believe. This is what her mother *says*, promises her, that Bedelia will live forever in one form or another. Fran never believes that Bedelia died. Bedelia can't die, she'd never allow it. Bedelia has too many angry bones in her body to die peacefully like other people, lie in the ground and just *stay* there.

Fran is her accident, Bedelia always says, you're my accident and thank God you were a girl. Boy accidents are too hard to control, Bedelia says, don't marry off so easily.

Bedelia planned on being a nun, she tells Fran, before she had her accident, even makes it as far as the convent gates before her father grips her by the upper arm and swings her in the direction of their Protestant home where the potatoes wait to be peeled and the table to be set.

You can be a teacher or a nurse or a wife if it's a career you want, says her father, but no goddamn nun.

So Bedelia teaches. Looks out the window at the Catholic church across the street when she teaches, then turns her back to the window to stare at the children in their desks. She is afraid of them, of their hairy skulls too big for their bodies, back-talking mouths. The principal tours Bedelia's class every so often; her work is impeccable, but she feels like an easy target, prey, a Canada goose during hunting season, X-marks-the-spot tattooed on her forehead, her back, her mouth. At times she feels she would be more fulfilled as a lizard. She would rather hide under a rock, her tongue flicking in and out, than teach.

She envies her mother's cat lying around all day, doing nothing but eating and chasing birds in the garden.

Sometimes Bedelia prays that she will be struck with laryngitis, mononucleosis, but illness will never eliminate the job, she'll still have to come back when she gets better. She wishes she were an animal in the zoo. Perhaps she already is an animal in a zoo, a passer-by just has to look in the classroom window and there she is, trapped in front of the children, her arms flailing wildly, her lips flapping pointlessly, her body turning circles and circles and circles from the board to the children to the board to the children like an armadillo trapped in a sandy-bottomed aquarium, while the children doodle and whisper among themselves, stare out the window and count down the minutes until freedom. Bedelia counts, too. Bedelia prancing up and down like a monkey in a floral-print dress trying to keep her audience, her keepers, engaged.

Bedelia stands in front of the class, day after day, the chalk gritty between her fingers. She hands out papers, takes back papers which after months of her useless prancing are nothing more than blank sheets.

One morning she turns to write on the board and has no words. Her arm, the chalk in her hand, reach out.

The chalk drives itself, leaves its trail over the board space, arches and swirls, crosses and bumps. Her arm follows the chalk, also swirls and crosses, bumps and screeches. She swirls and crosses, bumps and screeches, swirls and crosses, bumps and screeches; her arm stretches long and thin and blue, her face transparent and dissolving, and her body swells, bursts into water vapours, she evaporates before her students. They don't notice, they look forward to getting to leave early, or will they have to suffer a substitute?

She whirls in many pieces through the air, whirls and slides out the window, smoke, she will whirl and drift until nightfall, until her pieces reassemble and she condenses into a dew drop, coats the tip of a long blade of grass.

Back at home, she wraps up her dripping hair in a towel, throws her wet clothes into a pile and puts on her nightgown. Daddy, she announces, I've had enough.

One by one she carries her books to the burning fire-place, one by one cleans her book shelves, one by one discards her career as teacher. She will not, she has decided, be a teacher, a nurse, a wife, or a nun. She will do nothing. Absolutely nothing, a career choice that finally makes sense to her. Her family has money, why didn't she think of doing nothing before?

Bedelia resists until she is fifty-five, everyone's busy-at-doing-nothing spinster aunt and maybe even funny with her housekeeper the family thinks, until the arrival of Fran. The summer she turns fifty-five, Bedelia drinks too much punch at an engagement party for her niece and loses her virginity in the back garden, behind the garden shed, with the charming young priest visiting from Thunder Bay.

Now that she has reached her fifty-fifth birthday Bedelia believes she is safe from being impregnated, as does the young priest. Having sex with the priest, she feels, is the next best thing to becoming the nun she wanted to be. Besides, she loves the sound of an Ontario accent.

The priest loves women over fifty, likes his women mature and capable and not pregnable. He especially loves Bedelia's hair, her long smooth hands, her size eleven and a half triple A feet. He has been having doubts about staying in the priesthood lately anyway, but he doesn't want to upset his mother.

Soon after the priest's visit, Bedelia throws up regularly, every day. Breaks wind and belches, craves pickles dipped in brown sugar. The beginning of the end, she thinks, dares not think, she keeps cinching in the waists of her dresses and skirts more and more tightly, until the housekeeper opens her big mouth, says to Bedelia, You're pregnant, stop pretending you aren't.

The horror of the word.

Bedelia doesn't contact the priest, never speaks to him again — she felt embarrassed enough the morning after when she woke up with a headache and no hymen. Besides, if she were to tell him, he would just want to hang around, force her into making decisions she might not want to make. That would be out of the question.

He's done enough poking around, Bedelia tells her housekeeper, and the housekeeper pats her hand reassuringly.

Bedelia tries hot baths, scalds her thighs, the skin on her arms and belly. She vomits and curses after drinking glass after glass of gin especially purchased by the housekeeper. Bedelia contemplates throwing herself down the stairs but is afraid of the pain, afraid of breaking one of her fifty-five-year-old bones. Having a baby is probably less dangerous than cracking her skull on the hard steps. She feels she is too old for such gymnastics anyway. In the fifth month she hits her stomach once, twice, as hard as she can, but only winds herself and starts to cry. She can't dislodge this thing, this accident in her womb, can't simply stick her finger down her throat and vomit it out. Time to give up. She looks out the window at the grey clouds which roll like the tiny fluid animal in her stomach, watches rain pour abruptly and sharply from the sky.

Bedelia walks out the back door and into the blades of rain, rests her back against the wall of her house, in the garden. Lets the rain fall all over her, seep into her clothes, her ears, dribble through her hair. She sinks to the ground, huddles in the slick dirt.

Face pattered and spattered with rain, rain pounds into her eyes, drizzles into her mouth. She sighs, spreads her legs out in a V, lets her arms dangle in the muck. Single brown ants move slowly up her legs and arms; her hair rebels against the combs holding it in place and puffs out in the dampness and the rain. Her slender hands — her best feature, the priest said over a thin china cup of tea — trail in the mud, grow thin and green, and shine in the wetness. Her belly explodes, a bushy clump of leaves and stems.

Buds round as marbles appear, baby fists, at the tips of Bedelia's fingers, at the ends of stalks sprouted from her centre. Pop open into blossoms sweet and full, pink and white bundles amid the green, Bedelia's fingers and stalks bob and wave, full and fine as magic wands.

The housekeeper runs from the farthest part of the garden where she was frantically taking in the washing. Her feet pound across the grass, the ground rumbles with her steps, her breath steams out panicked and heavily. She pulls Bedelia from the ground and slaps the leaves where Bedelia's face used to be.

This just won't do, pants the housekeeper. This won't do at all, stand up and be a man, take responsibility for your actions, face the music. You've made your bed now lie in it lie in it lie in it! The housekeeper shakes Bedelia, shakes until the leaves fall away and reveal the tired and frightened woman inside the shrub.

The Blessed Virgin Mary did it, says the housekeeper, I suppose you can too. You have money and you have me. Running away is the coward's way. We'll raise her together. Your baby will be our pride and she will be our joy.

Bedelia looks sadly at the brown, wet face of her housekeeper, Bedelia's hair wet and still puffy as peonies, but she nods and lets herself be led to the house, into a nice warm bath, and then into a nice warm bed. She sleeps and sleeps, her hands on her stomach. Her mind makes itself up, thread winding around a spool.

Bedelia arrives at the family Easter brunch seven and a half months pregnant in an oversized dress, her stomach round as a tortoise's shell. A modern medical miracle.

Vesta is eating with us, announces Bedelia, and after an awkward pause, another place is set. The housekeeper sits down graciously, spreads her skirt thoughtfully over her knees. Vesta is not stupid, she knows she is unwelcome, but to hell with them all, this baby in Bedelia's stomach is hers too, which makes Vesta a member of the family. She picks up her fork and begins to eat. Eat and eat and eat. Eating for two.

Bedelia homes in on the nearest baby. Pats the baby's knees, strokes the baby's cheeks, pries open the baby's mouth and peers at the gums, down the throat, at the small wriggling fish of a tongue.

Do you want to hold her? asks the baby's mother, a woman thirty years younger than Bedelia. The mother drapes a dish towel over Bedelia's shoulder, settles her baby into Bedelia's arms.

They grow so quickly, says the mother.

Do they, says Bedelia as she arranges the baby carefully over the round shelf of her stomach. Bedelia and Vesta cluck over the baby admiringly, but know secretly that *their* baby will of course be superior. Vesta pops a sliver of fried ham into her mouth, chews, then offers the chewed ham to the baby. The baby's mouth opens, an electric garage door, and the baby swallows the ham. Vesta and Bedelia beam at the family seated around the table.

121

Bedelia holds the baby cautiously all through that Easter brunch, aware of the cloud of urine and baby powder surrounding them both, and she sneezes. Her relatives watch her, watch her stomach, her fingers stroking the baby's stomach inquisitively. None of the relatives would dare say anything. Bedelia, the unofficial, do-nothing queen wasp of the family nest, does what she wants, when she wants, and how she wants.

Outside the family, however, Bedelia is forced to poke her umbrella at little boys who waddle behind her in the street.

Her friends no longer come to call.

Too busy, they say.

But Bedelia doesn't let other people's petty politics bother her, she and Vesta are too busy planning for the baby, choosing wallpaper for the nursery, getting the crib ready.

Fran is born with teeth and thick black hair. The baby clutches avidly at Bedelia's breasts for milk, Bedelia who only nine months before suddenly realized she had breasts when the priest from Thunder Bay pointed them out to her with moist fingertips.

Fran grows up an accident, spills things, trips over nothing throughout her life until her knees and elbows are knotted with scars.

Your father was a holy man, says Bedelia. That's all you have to know.

Vesta rolls her eyes. Hole in the head more like it, she grumbles. Arranges chocolate-chip cookies on a plate and pours out three glasses of lemonade.

You girls come have a snack, she calls, and waits for Bedelia and Fran to come sit with her at the small table on the back porch.

Vesta holds out her arms and Fran runs and jumps into Vesta's lap. No other girl Fran knows has two such loving mothers.

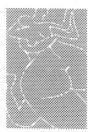

Squatting in the bushes peeing her life away — Bedelia's great-grandmother Fontana has a bladder the size of a pea. This makes Fontana sad, that she isn't capable of better self-control. Often she gripes and complains about her condition, but she has no choice. Of course, there is no sweeter sensation than a pee that's been kept in until it's ripe, but it's different when you have no choice. Forced to leave the room at inopportune times, when company is over, in the middle of dinner, Fontana treks to the back of the house and pees, the outhouse just a few too many yards away. The doctor says Fontana has an infection. Ladies of breeding would never pee in the bushes, but release themselves tidily in a chamber pot, or find a good and solid outhouse, the door discreetly latched behind them, but Fontana has no choice, she has no choice. Good, clean and convenient bushes are the vessel she prefers; her bladder waits for no man.

Fontana has to gather up her skirts one important dinner and find her way outside quickly, nature calls her just as the *fine roast chickens are being served, and she pees and pees and pees oh sweet relief and there she is, face to face with a bear cub, and her mouth opens in a sharp and silent O, the bear cub's mother big as the sky, madder than hell, Fontana's body frightened to stone, her blood turns to water and still she spurts, bear cub and mother guzzle from her spreading pool and shamble off. Her life saved, metamorphosis the happy alternative to being some bear's scratching post. Fontana planted in the ground forever now, watches the land around her shift: chopped and tamed, mown and watered, she listens to horse-drawn carriages click clack through the street followed by the roar of automobiles and airplanes leaving streaks of white smoke in the sky.*

Gargoyle heads carved and hung from her arms and throat. Stone jewels.

She spurts sweeter and sweeter relief, settles comfortably into the soft ground, enjoys the coolness of moss growing on her stone sides.

Lovers throw pennies that clank on her tiles. They look down into her pool of water, hold hands and kiss, sometimes do more than kiss and she splashes cold water on them, all in good fun. The pennies they have paid dot the bottom of her basin, she does her best to make their wishes come true.

Happy to oblige, she bubbles. Lucky to be alive.

Fran's own skin burns red and rough, the nurses rub on coating after coating of lotions, oils, then steroid ointments. Lymph oozes from where her skin cracks from dryness, in the bends of her elbows, behind her knees, the corners of her lips. It's the itching she can't stand, the itch of a thousand mosquitoes beneath her skin; crystals of dried lymph stick to the sites of the sharpest itches. Fran sighs, so softly, the skin on her chest bursts open with the smooth tear of rubber. She opens her new-born eyes, blink blink, clamours and bites her way out of the human tissue of the dead body, claws and rips up through the chest, her head the first part of her to emerge, her shoulders, then the rest of her wet magpie self.

Fran crouches on her human remains, she is now the size and the shape of a magpie, but instead of a magpie head and chest, her human face and breasts remain, slick with freshly hatched wetness. Fran is not a magpie like her mother, but a new-born harpy, her parts unreconciled, her transformation incomplete. Not yet done with life.

She peers at the collapsed body in the bed, her old shell, her discarded pelt. Stretches the muscles in her arms, stringy biceps and shrunken forearms, stretches her neck and tries to fly off the bed but only succeeds in flapping awkwardly to the cold, hard tiles of the floor. She bumps into a metal cabinet, then plumps down for a short rest.

Fran waddles to the window, the sill too high, so she flaps onto the seat of a chair, then jumps up on the sill. Chews at the itch of new feathers on her belly, her back. One wing stretches, an elaborate fan, the other wing stretches, they both flap, tuck back to her sides. Her stomach wails with hunger, her back is to the partly opened window, and the floor leads nowhere except into cold metal objects. So she takes a breath, then dives, spreading her arms widely and strongly.

The harpy who was Fran glides from the room, flies away from the hospital, Griffin and God. Nurses cluster around her hollowed body.

She enjoys her wings, her face pebbled with rain, does figure eights, air ballet, dives along the surfaces of streets, park grass, river and lake water; she has never stretched her neck so long, been so free of pain. She kill-shakes a runaway poodle by the scruff of the neck, not because she wants to, but because it's in her nature. When she was a woman, she always liked poodles, those teacup poodles, the size of a Kleenex box, just the right size to cradle in her arms, in between her breasts. She brought home a poodle puppy once, saw it through the window of the pet shop next to the grocery store. The poodle looked at her through the window and the song, "How much is that doggie in the window?" whistled through her head.

She brought the puppy up the steps of her house, she was happy and sweaty, giggly, but as soon as Griffin saw the dog he began to sneeze, sneezed and sneezed and sneezed so much she was sure he'd pop a blood vessel. She had to return the dog, took back her money sternly, vacuumed dog hair off the seats in the car and never thought about the puppy again.

She guts with her talons, burrows her face with a sharp dip and a sigh and leaves the poodle's body by the road like so much roadkill.

For a time Fran lives fiercely, scrounges for meat behind restaurants and grocery stores, eats squirrels, grounded birds, runaway domestic pets. Her woman's face and bosom white white white as cream, her nipples and eyes dark and luminous as old coffee. Griffin would never recognize her. His own mother.

She still hasn't forgotten she was a woman. This is her trouble. She sniffs the air and glides, glides in the direction of her boy.

Carmen approaches Griffin calmly, methodically, as she would a wounded rabbit. In order to save him from himself.

I, she thinks, am your destiny. You are too dumb to know what's good for you.

I'm sorry about your mother, Griffin, she says. I'm sorry I said she was trying to manipulate our lives. I'm sorry I called her a racist. You know I didn't mean it.

She affects a pathetic and hurt tone, How could you think I meant such a thing? I would never say anything to hurt you. Of course deep down I *loved* your mother.

Griffin hoes the dirt in the patch behind an office building, hoes around Carmen's black suede shoes rooted in the crumbly layer of top soil. He has been instructed to plant ornamental kale and petunias. He would rather plant herbs: chervil, sage, maybe thyme. Time after time, he whistles quietly, sucks the air inward. He knows he could do a killer herb garden. Could colour-match tiny blossoms perfectly.

Griffin plants, his eyes trace worms and weed roots, sweat springs out of his skin moist as the dirt is wet. He never planted anything for his mother. He wonders if she would have noticed if he had. He taps the soil down around a white, double-headed petunia.

Griffin is engaged to Renata. Renata wears spectacles and Birkenstocks, doesn't shave her armpits or her legs. She is Caucasian, his mother would approve. His eyes flicker once over Carmen's smooth smooth legs, warm as milk chocolate. He doesn't hear what she says, rattling on as though he could be convinced to change his mind. His mother died for him. His mother died, he made her die. He didn't do enough; for once he will do enough.

Griffin gets his hair cut and buys a new suit for the wedding. It's going to be a quiet civil ceremony, he's decided, not the three-ring tuxedo circus Carmen planned, but he still wants things to look professional.

Griffin? asks Carmen, her feet follow him into the kale bed. Are you listening to me? Hellooo, she says. Griffin, wake up.

You gonna get your hair done for the wedding? he asks Renata. A flower in your hair would look really nice.

Am I going to do what?

He takes her to a florist and she sits for over an hour, staring at hundreds of stiff pages of hairy flower arrangements.

She agrees to have a flat white orchid in her hair.

We could add some satin ribbon and pearl strands, suggests the florist.

Good idea, chirps Griffin.

Kiss my ass, Renata wants to say. No thank you, she says, I don't think so. Oh, I don't think that's necessary.

Her eyes pop out at the price of the flower, but Griffin writes out a cheque for the deposit with a flourish.

He helps her pick out a dress, a lacy mini-dress to show off her legs, but it's got a traditional top, and he buys her underwear from that lingerie shop in the trendy part of town. Renata looks gorgeous in anything, but he really likes those boob-pusher corset things. With garters, man, those look good. White lace, black looks too sleazy. Carmen used to wear black underwear.

You want me to wear *this?* says Renata. She fastens the garter belt half-heartedly around her waist and looks doubtfully in the mirror.

Griffin can see the edge of Carmen's black slip peeping out from the bottom hem of her skirt.

Excuse me, he says. Could you please not step on the plants. He pulls out a packet of thyme seeds and sprinkles the seed in the freshly dug dirt. He refuses to look into Carmen's eyes. He looks at Carmen's feet, her chin.

Griffin, why are you ignoring me? asks Carmen. I have feelings too, you know.

He addresses and mails out invitations for the post-ceremony party. Only some fancy snacks, not an actual dinner; they have almost no money because the plane tickets cost so much. Back to Portugal for their honeymoon. Griffin's stomach seizes every time he thinks about Portugal. He's insisted on sleeping on the couch for two weeks before the wedding so that when they're married it'll be like the first time again.

When they are more financially secure, in about five years he estimates, because that's when he'll finish off his undergraduate and graduate degrees, he will watch with pride and amazement as Renata gives birth to their first baby; he figures he'll be able to cope with Renata's screaming in the delivery room and transition or whatever it's called, such a gentle person she is generally, how bad can transition get? The baby will be a boy named Italo, or if it's a girl Romana. Romaine lettuce has always been his favourite. If Fran were alive, she'd insist on Margaret as a name, Marg for short. This is what she would have named Griffin had he been a girl. Maybe Romana's middle name could be Margaret.

Griffin sees a tear hang from Carmen's chin. The tear drops onto the fabric of her blouse.

He bows his head down to the ground, to the rich dirt, to the scattered thyme seeds he won't deliberately plant but which he makes sure are in the best growing conditions possible.

Carmen's feet leave the kale bed and the high heels of her shoes press small round holes into the grass.

Carmen's mum Pascale used to have arms, eyes, and a gentle disposition, just like other mums. Carmen's mum Pascale tried to hold down a part-time job as a registered nurse at the hospital and be a normal mother to her babies, a normal wife to her husband; but then came the day she threw in the towel.

She throws towels into the laundry hamper, throws them in with the skill of a professional, but turns from her towels when she hears the bleat of a baby, her eldest baby Carmen, teetering on the edge of the stairs in her little wheeled cart, Carmen about to plunge down a flight of stairs. Carmen's mum knows it will take at least five seconds to reach the cart at the top of the stairs. Five seconds no human feet can make it in.

Carmen's mum Pascale screams, brings her hands up to her face; she screams so loudly her body shakes itself awake and, as quickly and efficiently as a whip, her third arm snaps out, *stretches, and pulls the baby and cart back to safety. Breathes a sigh of relief and let's all just go have a big glass of milk and some peanut butter cookies to soothe our nerves.*

Pascale keeps her special arm in reserve. Understandably enough, she'll bring it out only on special occasions — sometimes at parties when she's feeling a little giddy. She doesn't want the local news to get a hold of such a thing. She's not a freak, she's just trying to be a good mother, a good wife, a good employee. No, she says, my extra arm is nothing special.

The eyes in the back of Pascale's head make their debut performance when she is preparing meat loaf in the kitchen — her special meat loaf made with fried onions and garlic — the onions and elephant garlic frying on the stove, Carmen's little brother reaching up up up with his puppy-fat arms to the handle of the frying pan. Suddenly he is jerked away from the stove and given a sharp smack on the bottom, all while Pascale chops carrots on the cutting board, her back to him the whole time, but her brand new eyes, one green, one black, peer through the hair on the back of her head, and her third elastic arm works overtime.

Pascale, the miracle mum.

Pascale works at the General Hospital. Near the end of a night shift she is tired and impatient, Don't give me any shit, she says to her patients, it's been a long fucking night. One more hour and a new nurse'll be on, so just don't give me any grief.

Mrs. Seltzer's mouth snakes out and bites Pascale's arm as Pascale hands Mrs. Seltzer her pills. Pascale shakes with fury, her brain's circuits speeding up, speeding up, and the skin around her neck rises in a glorious crest, Mrsss. Ssseltzzzer, she hisses, baring her teeth, and her tongue flicks once before the skin on her neck settles back to normal, before the fork of her slick, long tongue melts, retreats into its original, soft shape. Pascale calls for a porter because suddenly Mrs. Seltzer's turned to stone, transformed by Pascale's basilisk glare, from pinky cheeked old-lady-flesh into a hunk of stone that will eventually dissolve into nothing but a heap of gravel. All the nurses applaud when Mrs. Seltzer is carted from the room in a wheelbarrow, while the rest of Pascale's patients sit up cooperative and attentive. Pascale sets her cap straight and gets back to work.

Pascale, the miracle nurse.

Oh, she says, it's nothing, nothing special.

Renata's job, Griffin says, is to organize the food for the wedding reception. She arranges for a Caribbean caterer from the restaurant down the street and saves money by chopping up the snack vegetables herself; every night for half a week she cleans and chops carrots, celery, cherry tomatoes, and stores them in buckets of water first in the fridge, then around the apartment. The night before the wedding she will arrange them in wagon wheel patterns on platters, and the morning of the wedding Griffin and a friend will take them to the house where the party is. But Griffin has problems with the menu.

Caribbean? What kind of food is that? asks Griffin. How about cold cuts and buns? What about corned beef?

She hates corned beef. Memories of corned beef have kept Renata a vegetarian. Corned beef in packets her friend Karim's mother buys at the grocery store and pops into boiling water. Corned beef she is forced to eat as a kid.

You never used to eat meat, Renata says. Why meat all of a sudden?

Renata's family has always been vegetarian, but for her entire grade three year, the year her grandmother is sick, she eats lunch at her friend Karim's house.

Nice hot lunch, Karim's mother says on corned beef days, and the water the corned beef is boiled in, weakly salty with bubbles of grease, drains from the meat and soaks into her bread; nice hot lunch now cold and soggy lunch. Renata takes a bite of the rapidly disintegrating sandwich too big for her suddenly very little mouth, her lips narrow as the slit in a mailbox. The frightened tips of her teeth show, the pieces of sandwich resting on her plate crack and crumble and slip slip she eats the sandwich in tiny bites, slips it into her mouth in crumbs. Soggy bread coats her tongue, the cooled salty beef chew chew, then painful swallow then sip milk, chew chew, swallow splash the milk — then it happens the way it always does, the beef in her mouth half-chewed still connected by a long and stubborn string of fat, umbilical cord, to a bite of beef already in her stomach. Swallow swallow, swallow swallow, and still the string there, the meat on either side of her throat going neither up nor down. She imagines pulling at the string in her mouth and bringing up the beef, her sandwich, rivulets of milk and coils of intestine.

Why aren't you eating? asks Karim's mother. Don't you know there are little children starving in Africa? When my mother was your age that corned beef sandwich would have been like Christmas to her. She would have thanked her lucky stars for a hot corned beef sandwich. All my grandmother could afford was lard sandwiches. Maybe if you have to eat a lard sandwich or two you'll smarten up.

Evenings on corned-beef-for-lunch days Renata cries until her face is soggy, falls to sleep ashamed and afraid because she knows she will be in trouble if her parents know she eats meat, because of the starving children, and because of Karim's grandmother's lard sandwiches. She hiccups and burps up the odour of shame and corned beef.

No, Renata says to Griffin. No fucking corned beef.

Griffin has changed. This is not the Griffin she met and fell in love with in Europe. The Griffin she came back to Canada for would have wanted to get married on a mountain or in a meadow, a private ceremony with no one but the two of them and the sky and the mountain attending. This wedding ceremony seems unnecessary to her. Too status quo. Something it sounds like his ex-girl-friend, Carmen, would have insisted on. Renata doesn't think that she and Carmen can like each other much. Once she and Griffin ran into her and an old friend of Griffin's, Kevin, in front of a movie theatre. Carmen didn't say much, just kept her hand firmly on Kevin's elbow and everyone was very polite, but Carmen couldn't keep her eyes off Renata's hair. It became so obvious it was almost embarrassing, so Renata pulled the hood of her coat over her head and then Carmen and Kevin stomped away through the snow. She wonders how Carmen and Griffin ever got along as a couple. Maybe Carmen consumed large amounts of meat and animal products too. This meat thing bothers Renata. Griffin started eating meat shortly after his mother died. Renata finds wizened strips of left-over beef jerky in his pockets. For dinner on his way home from work, he gulps down fast-food burgers, fried chicken and french fries. When Renata and Griffin shop for gro-ceries, Griffin throws packages of luncheon meat and thick, bloody steaks into their grocery cart. At breakfast, his cheeks bulge with strips of bacon, not even tofu substi-tute bacon but real bacon made from *pigs*. Or he rolls around fried sausages in the frying pan, scoops them into his mouth before they even have a chance to hit the plate. He carries a jar of bacon bits to work in his backpack and sprinkles the bits over salads. Once she catches him sprin-kling them over a bowl of cereal.

At night, before he decides to sleep on the couch, she feels like she is getting into bed with a six-foot-four pep-peroni stick, warm and greasy with meat fat. His skin is so salty it sets her teeth on edge just to kiss him, and his face, his face is the pink of a cured Easter ham from being in the sun all day. She worries about melanoma and secretly monitors his moles for changes.

She tries for months to wean him off this meat-only diet until one night he begins to weep over a bowl of sunflower seed and carrot soup.

Do you believe in ghosts? he asks.

Why? She peers into his soup.

This soup smells like my mother.

The carroty vapour in her nose twists into the distinct smell of blood running from an under-cooked roast beef.

Long tears drip down the sides of his nose, dangle and cloud at the tip.

Renata doesn't even bother to tell her parents she's getting married to a meat-eater. Later maybe. She hates being fussed over and she doesn't want to face their disappointment. She tells Griffin her parents left on an around-the-world trip. Won't be back for at least a year.

Fran butts her head against the New Boss's office window so hard the glass bends. She pecks at the glass with her teeth, her head cocked to one side, and spits poison, not because she wants to, but because she can't help it.

The New Boss masturbates at his desk; even from the outside she can hear his soft moans, smell the pillowed odour of dissipated farts and old cologne characteristic of his office, his skin. So lonely he is. He dabs himself with a Kleenex, stuffs the Kleenex in the waste basket, pushes once at the papers on his desk, then once again. "Fran" he doodles in the margins. He pushes his glasses farther over the bone in the middle of his nose.

The night before the wedding Renata and Griffin are supposed to have their friends over for drinks and snacks and vegetable arranging. The friends will go home early. This is what Griffin has planned. After work, though, he goes to the Keg for a beer just to get his gears going again after so many petunias. He nurses the beer, looks at himself in the mirror behind the bar. His glasses make him look smarter, he thinks, downright scholarly.

Maybe he should change his major when he goes back to school in the winter and study in a field more practical than philosophy, maybe this would be the right choice what with being a husband and a future father, accountable and responsible. He watches the bartender absentmindedly, the rippled, smooth skin on her chest as she mixes drinks, pops celery sticks into Caesars like a juggler.

Hey, he says. Can I go down on you?

She glances at him once, then back at the row of half-filled glasses on the bar. She juggles Caesars and Bloody Marys.

Okay, he says sliding off his chair. You think about it. I'll be back at about eleven, okay?

Renata chops carrots and celery, arranges pickles, dill and sweet, on the first platter in a wagon-wheel pattern. Rinses the last of the cherry tomatoes, some round and small as marbles, drains them in the colander, pats them dry with a checkered dishcloth and pops one in her mouth. She bites firmly, feels the tickle of juice and tomato seeds spurt on the inside of her cheek. A little leaks out between her lips and dots the linoleum.

She locks the door behind her. Today, the day before her wedding, she is a woman of purpose, unperturbed by the fact that Griffin hasn't come home yet even though he said he'd be home early to help with the vegetables. This is how she gives him his space, by remaining unperturbed. Chooses to understand only those things he tells her explicitly. No games, they promised each other. No games.

Renata is from Kamloops and Griffin has perfect eye-sight. This is what they tell each other when they decide to come clean, the time she finds out that Griffin's glasses aren't real. These were some of the games that had to be cleared up before they could agree to live together. True love, they agree, requires truth and trust. Living together is different from a casual affair; bad habits and awkward secrets have to be revealed on both sides before the final commitment is made.

Before she gives them up for Griffin, Renata is an expert at games.

When she is eighteen, she touches a girl's breast on a dare, she can never resist a dare, runs her sweaty thumb over the nipple, looks at the blue veins and feels the creamy weight. The girl and her breast become a site for Renata's anger, people think she's some kind of lez, they don't understand it was just a *dare*, until the girl gets married, sends a letter to the class reunion committee that says she has a baby and a half somewhere in the Kootenays.

Renata's anger collapses into nostalgia and she covets the thought of that girl's stomach, the round smooth bulge, expanding breasts, even the morning sickness. She would love to experience morning sickness, touch her own stomach with the flat of her hands and feel the hard nut of a foetus. But she doesn't want a teenager. Teenagers scare her, *being* a teenager scared her, the loss of control over her body, her mind. She remembers teenagehood as though it were a long long illness.

Renata sticks to being an expert at young men, knowing the games and words they want to hear. She learns these games when she teaches English in Spain for a year and meets Guillermo, then in Greece spends time with Trevor from Texas and becomes Renata from Reno. In Paris she gets sick from the pollution and the rain and no one cares about Texas so she becomes Renata from Kamloops once again.

In London she looks at paintings of Queen Elizabeth the First, marvels at the hair just like her own, wonders if Queen Elizabeth had a black ancestor. Beautifully unman-ageable hair, studded, no caked, with jewels.

At the hostel in Lisbon she meets Italo, and she pre-tends she is from Spain. Smooth and tall Italo, obviously fresh off the boat from Canada. With his round owl spec-tacles he looks just like a professor, and in bed he is satis-factory plus. Italo brings her the closest she has ever come in her life to what she imagines an orgasm feels like.

Just coming this close is enough, she reassures him. My inability to achieve orgasm has nothing to do with your technique.

She tries on his glasses for fun, the bridge drops over her nose, and her sight remains unchanged.

They're fake, says Italo.

I'm not Spanish, says Renata.

Is Renata your real name?

Yes. She runs her tongue along his jaw. Is Italo your real name?

Maybe.

In Germany, Renata and Italo-Griffin walk the cobble-stoned streets of small villages where he buys her cheap silver jewellery and she buys him a CD from a small record shop.

Who's this? he asks. He turns the CD over in his hands, peers through his lenses at the face on the CD cover.

Billie Holiday. You've never heard of Billie Holiday? She's the greatest singer who ever lived.

I don't have a CD player, he says.

Well. Just look at the cover then, I guess. Or read the lyrics. I'll mail you a tape when I go back home.

Her hero is Billie Holiday, Lady Day. At home on her parents' stereo in Kamloops, she listens and listens with her hair poised like antennae.

In Nuremberg they drink foamy beer in a smoky pub from tall, thick glasses. Other customers' dogs stick their muzzles in Griffin and Renata's crotches, try to carry away the food on their plates and dig in their backpacks stuffed with bread and soft, vegetarian-cheese.

Maybe you could come visit me in Canada, says Griffin.

Oh yeah? she says. They share a Camel even though neither of them smoke.

That would be fabulous, she says. Noch ein bier?

What?

I already come from Canada. Isn't that fabulous? Her eyes beery and bright.

If she weren't so beautiful, he would walk out and catch the train to Munich like his original plan. Instead, he decides, *Renata,* not Carmen, is the woman he should marry.

Renata used to be an expert on young men from Spain. Now she is pretty much retired and from Kamloops.

She drives the truck to the florist to buy the flower hairpiece then speeds to the liquor store for the two cases of cheap champagne. Renata smiles at the woman at the cash register, who smiles back — they recognize each other. Renata's only been here a million times before. She is the only customer in the store.

I like your perfume, says the cashier. Smells like ferns.

The cashier hoists the champagne cases onto the counter.

Thanks, says Renata. She doesn't wear perfume, maybe it's the scent of the soap she uses. Still it's nice of the cashier to say this, strange of her to say this. Renata can smell the cashier's rich warm flesh, the sweat sprinkled on her nose, her forehead, in her armpits. The cashier is a beautiful woman. Renata has never seen anyone so polished outside of the pages of a fashion magazine.

I like yours too, she says, boldly, Can I smell? and she stretches her neck out to the cashier.

The space between them shrinks, becomes tangible and strange as the cashier leans forward. Renata smells her, smells her shampoo, her breath, the light down on her skin. Then the cashier pulls away, looks at Renata, and Renata blushes. She pays for the champagne and her skin yelps as she walks farther and farther away holding one of the cases until the automatic door opens and she exits into the parking lot. She loads the case onto the floor of the truck.

She walks back to the store for the second case of champagne, falters to a stop in front of a woman and her bucket of flowers in front of the store. Renata's legs fingers teeth mouth manipulate and stretch; she wants to buy a rose. It is difficult to form the words.

One please, she whispers. So quietly she can barely hear herself. She enters the liquor store again, circles to the cash register, holds out the flower.

Here, she says.

Here.

Men and women are always giving the cashier at the liquor store flowers from the door. These women and men are easy to spot; they come to the store over and over again, first buy regular booze, then start buying souvenir corkscrews or lousy wine they ask her opinion of.

Lousy, the cashier says. Try this one.

Or if they know their wines and don't need her help or haven't thought of this strategy, they pretend to browse among the tiny bottles of hard liquor in the basket by her cash register. These men and women small talk with the cashier about the weather, the parking, how convenient the little bottles of hard liquor are.

Rip off, she says. Let's keep the line moving.

They quickly buy the small bottle of Glenfiddich, or Beefeater, or Chivas Regal, then walk out and the woman with the bucket of flowers at the door makes a killing and the cashier has one more drooping rose or smelly bundle of carnations under her counter.

The cashier is on a vacation from relationships; she is always gracious with the flowers but never gives anything more than a thank you and a business-like smile and tucks the flower away where it sags and dies. Soon she will have to ask to be relocated again. Too many people in love-at-first-sight with her.

What's your name? asks the cashier.

Renata.

You smell like ferns, Renata. And she takes the rose, kisses it, then gives it back. This is for you, Mika says.

And Mika isn't even supposed to be working that night.

Lucky thing.

This is where we met, Renata and Mika will say. This is the booze you bought, this is what I was wearing and this is what I was thinking when you said that. Renata will blush, still apprehensive of Mika's caresses and light kisses even in the protective dark of the street.

Lucky thing.

Lucky thing.

Mika wasn't supposed to work that night, but Joan was, poor Joan, 3:35 P.M., Friday afternoon, her voice soft and sad on the phone to Mika, Meek, she says, can you fill in for me tonight? I'm very sick. Please can you do me this favour? And of course Mika says yes, who couldn't to such a soft sad voice.

Of course, says Mika, are you all right? And Joan just sighs because she doesn't feel up to saying anything else. Words too elusive, too uncertain.

10:35 A.M., Friday morning, Joan lays her favourite orange towel on the grass in the backyard, spreads it smooth, coats her body with suntan lotion, then lies down on her stomach and smiles with one side of her mouth at the sun.

The sun blasts her shoulder blades, the backs of her thighs, the side of her face. Sweat bubbles up to the surface of her skin, smooth and salty as meat fat, moisture on her stomach soaks into the towel, and her edges — the tips of her fingers, her toes, the points of her elbows, the unprotected rim of her ear — begin to curl and spit. Sizzle and pop, fry fry fry, it's that kind of day.

Hairs on her arms, her legs, the back of her neck, bleach blonde and blonder, stand up straighter and straighter, bake sharp and white as thistles as thorns.

Joan's mind wanders as she sleeps, crawls over the towel, through the grass, by-passes the peeping heads of earthworms, vibrant colonies of ants. Joan's mind wanders through mounds of litter, over piles of gravel while Joan's sleeping body browns and bakes; her pigments flower until her skin is tough as a rind — the sun feels so darn good, the sun strokes her further into sleep, lifts moisture from her body, dehydrates her. Her dry tongue oozes from the corner of her mouth; it's so damn hot, her tongue stretches and lengthens, burrows through the towel, through the grass and into the soil, past all roots, deep deep and deeper, her tongue the obstinate root of a cactus, her flesh shrunk and bound in cactus pelt.

3:10 P.M., Joan's mother peers out the window. Screams. She runs into the garden, rips Joan's tongue out of the ground, shreds her skin on her daughter's thorns, but plucks her daughter from the earth goddammit, lifts her daughter high into the air, dashes into the house and dumps Joan into the tub, cold water and shower curtain shade. This is what mothers are capable of in crises.

I think you should call in sick today, says Joan's mum. You're not in any state to work. I'll get the phone, you call someone to take your place.

And Joan whispers into the phone held to her ear by her mum, whispers for Mika to fill in for her, please don't tell the boss; this'll be her third time sick this month.

Joan sighs, settles into the cool water in the tub, weeps softly and vows never never never again to sunbathe.

Now how about a nice cup of flat ginger ale? her mum says, soaks a rag in ice water and lays it on her daughter's spiky forehead.

Four A.M. and Renata swishes her hands in hot dish water. Detergent suds trap in the fine hairs on her arms. What has she done? What is she doing? For the first time ever she is all of one piece.

Four A.M. and Renata washes the dishes, wipes clean sudsy glasses because what else is there to do when it's four A.M., tomorrow is your wedding day and you've just had your very first orgasm on top of one hundred bottles of beer? She can't sleep to save her life even if her life were worth saving, even if she appreciated and cared for Griffin the way she should. She stares at Griffin sleeping on the couch under a sheet for a long long time. Watches the rise and fall of his chest, the gleam of his eyelids in the dark. She closes the door to the kitchen softly. Sweet and lovely, trusting Griffin.

Although she scrubs her face and her body the moment she gets home, she can still smell Mika on her skin, see her between her fingers. Also between her fingers she sees fear and suspicion, and lust pure and deep as water. Lust eats holes into her brain — a film cell melted and burnt into a hole on the movie screen, the sarcastic cheer of the crowd because how's the projectionist gonna fix this one?

She knows that by getting married she is making the right decision. This is the normal thing to do, the accepted way; maybe she will even have a baby once she has thoroughly forgotten her own childhood. She knows that Griffin would like a baby badly, the sooner the better. He pays attention to children in public, sees baby clothes at friends' houses and asks, where's the baby? This tears her heart out. So sweet.

And what would be the alternative? Mika. She has no idea what the alternative, an unfinished space, is. She is sad to realize how much she desires safety, predictability.

Renata remembers an old friend of hers, a lesbian friend who was walking with her girlfriend in a mall. They were followed by a bunch of boys who chanted, dyke dyke dyke dyke dyke, then started throwing handfuls of gravel.

Dyke dyke dyke dyke dyke dyke dyke, they chanted, and no one came to help.

The tumbler cracks and bursts, hand inside it rotating with the dishcloth. Renata brings her fingers out of the water, a slice on one of the knuckles that was buried in Mika's hair. Blood slides out red and painless at first, then it gushes and she sees herself getting married in the morning, her hand bristling black stitches fine as fly's legs, her knuckle throbbing louder than her voice whispering the words *I do.*

The blood in Renata's body stops flowing the harder she thinks about her wedding day. Her fingers rest motionless above the water, her toes curl and sprout roots into the linoleum floor. The skin on her feet browns, hardens and wrinkles into bark that creeps up her legs. She forces herself to stop thinking of her wedding day, returns her thoughts to Mika, then shivers, bites feeling back into her hands. She shakes the bark off her shins and feet like bread crumbs. Not yet. Not now.

She winds gauze around her hand over and over and over.

Mika runs, leaps over gutters — it is after all a full moon and it is the day before her period begins, so of course nothing is normal. She skips and runs until she reaches the reception hall where her sister Isabelle methodically ties and glues gigantic wire and satin bows for the Finch-Hasmir wedding scheduled the day after tomorrow.

You wanna drink? calls Mika, and Isabelle nods so vigorously her hair falls into her eyes and stays there — but she has no time, she has no time to get the hair out of her eyes and get all these decorations done in time for two P.M. the day after tomorrow. Isabelle does have time for a sip of wine though. Her mouth begins to water.

Mika pours out two plastic cups of wine and the women sip, grateful for the sharp cut of the alcohol on the backs of their throats.

Decided to show up, eh? says Isabelle, and she passes boxes of ribbons, wire and tiny china doves to Mika.

Just got off work, says Mika.

You got off work two hours ago! says Isabelle. What, did you get lost on the way here?

Hmph.

Isabelle ties bows and peers through her fallen hair at Mika, who coils ribbon around the wire feet of a thousand china doves.

Waves, says the bride's mother. I want the ceiling to be a wash of waves on the seashore and at the crest of every wave, foam made of doves. You know what I mean don't you?

Of course, says Isabelle, and she smiles so hard she pops a blood vessel and her nose begins to bleed.

Waves, says the bride's mother, like this, and her hands gesture in a graceful waving movement.

Waves, says the mother, should also be in the centres of the tables and at the end of every pew. My daughter is an Olympic-calibre swimmer, you know. That is why we have chosen an underwater theme. Perhaps we could have ocean sounds during the dinner, and all of the servers can wear clothing reminiscent of the ocean too.

Mermaids, the mother continues brightly and holds up an index finger as though testing the air. Skirts and trousers with a sequined scale pattern. Do you think the waiters and waitresses would agree to having their faces painted blue like mermaids?

Isabelle smiles graciously in spite of bits of dried blood from her nosebleed crusted on her chin.

Blue skin shouldn't be that hard to accomplish, says Isabelle. But it will cost extra.

Mika and Isabelle spend all week modelling and painting starfish from papier mâché. At each table-centre will be an orderly mound of sand stuck with coral, a treasure map on antique-looking paper and a wave of doves draped with blue ribbon. At each place setting, a tiny treasure chest containing blue and green mints wrapped in net, of course, with a tiny scroll saying thank you from the bride and groom! What a panic. The wedding is the day after tomorrow.

The least you could do is come up with a decent excuse so I can know why I've had to make waves by myself all night, says Isabelle. Jesus Mika. Entertain me, I'm bored.

I've brought along my sister, says the mother of the bride. I hope you don't mind. We've decided that we want the bride and groom seated at the head table in matching scallop-shell seats. King and Queen of the Sea!

The aunt and mother of the bride nod at Isabelle, at each other.

Thrones, says the aunt. Scallop-shell thrones!

Isabelle rips apart bags of marbles bought at a bargain basement, small milky coloured marbles that could pass for large pearls. She scatters the pearls on the demo table centrepiece in front of the two women.

Pearls, says the mother, how clever! I hope they're not too expensive. Can you add some more coral to the centre-piece? I think we need more coral.

Isabelle scuffles through a box of tissue paper at the other end of the room, far away from the two women, but close enough to hear the mother of the bride say, Oriental people have a reputation for being good at math so I'm not going to worry. My accountant is Oriental too.

Isabelle stands up quickly as though a rod has shot up her back, but closes her mouth, thinks about the money she'll make from this wedding.

Orientals are great at math, thinks Isabelle and she jams another chunk of coral into the sand, scatters more pearls, hums busily to keep the blood from rushing to her head too quickly. In her head Isabelle tallies how the bags of marbles have shot up from fifty cents a bag to five dollars.

Isabelle has had three nosebleeds so far this month. Stupid people give her nosebleeds, a condition no doctor can help.

You should see this bride, says Isabelle to Mika. This bride plasters on so much make-up she probably wears lipstick on her vulva. Pass me the scissors.

So I finally allowed myself to be laid, says Mika.

You did what? You did what?

I met a woman, says Mika. A beautiful beautiful woman. Hottest woman you've ever seen, so hot her hair's red. Hot, says Mika. Hot.

Hot, repeats Isabelle.

Hot, says Mika. As in come-on-baby-light-my-fire hot.

Isabelle makes big eyes at Mika and drapes white imitation velvet over the back of a chair with a huge, scalloped back. Mika drinks from her glass of wine, belches.

And? says Isabelle. Cover your mouth when you burp. And? And and and and and? It's about time you got laid; nuns get more action than you.

Her name is Renata, says Mika. She's a regular at the store, we had fabulous sex in the back room. I gave her my number, she didn't give me hers. She has a boyfriend, you know the story. I can't believe I'm getting mixed up in a boyfriend thing, but this is one exceptional woman. Exceptional.

Boyfriend! says Isabelle. Boyfriend!

Actually husband-to-never-be, they're supposed to be getting married tomorrow — she has the reddest hair in the world.

You're prepared to be someone's mistress? asks Isabelle.

No. I'm not going to be anyone's mistress. It's not like we're *seeing* each other, but of course she can't go through with this marriage crap now that she's slept with a *girl.* She can't do that. How could she live with herself? Sleeping with me cancels out the wedding. Naturally.

Naturally, says Isabelle. Naturally you're joking I hope. How big a wedding? Did she tell you?

No. I didn't ask. Why should I care? I'm not in *love* or anything, I'm not waiting by the phone until she calls. She can do what she wants. Besides, she wouldn't go through with it. She's too sincere, I know it, and this guy she's marrying sounds like a dork.

I know the wedding business, says Isabelle, marbles and netting and china doves in her hands. People don't stop weddings for things like feelings or infidelity. Weddings are economic arrangements. Believe me, it's cheaper and a lot easier just to grit your teeth and go through with a wedding than it is to stop one. People don't like being invited to weddings that are cancelled, weddings where their gifts aren't appreciated. That's not the way it's done. The show must go on.

Married. Mika doesn't even know what this means. The onset of her period, Renata's perfume, the full moon, have confused her. Of course Mika's not in love with Renata or anything, of course Mika doesn't expect Renata to be in love with her. But Renata would never go through with the wedding now. Mika ties and glues blue and green wire bows, and coils ribbon around the feet of a china dove. Beyond the dressing up, the exchange of money and cake-mixers, what does marriage mean? She glances at the bow forming between her fingers, puts it down and chews on her thumb nail. Who in the hell does Renata think she is? Mika is hardly prepared to be some straight chick's experiment.

The one I feel sorry for is the husband, says Isabelle. He's in for a nasty surprise one day.

Renata's wedding ceremony, Mika's funeral, Renata's wedding reception, Mika's wake. Another tragic lesbian love story. Not that Mika is in love. Of course not. Of course not.

Her heart lies on its side and draws its knees up to its chin.

You all right? asks Isabelle.

Mika hiccups. She wipes her eyes on a wad of white tissue paper. Blows her nose. Not in love. Of course not. In lust maybe, but never in love.

Oh sweety, says Isabelle, and she puts down the velvet and wraps her arms around Mika's shoulders.

I'm *not* in love or anything, says Mika. She hugs Isabelle back tightly. Mika's secret tears soak into the fabric covering Isabelle's shoulder.

Stupid straight chicks.

Griffin sleeps so deeply he wakes himself with a snore. He squeezes his nostrils closed with his index finger and thumb and re-immerses his brain and body in sleep. He and his friends arranged vegetables far too long, way past eleven o'clock. So he missed his last chance to play at bachelor with the bartender at the Keg, and Renata didn't show up until late and on top of that, said she only had enough money to pay for one case of champagne.

At this same time tomorrow night, he'll be married. Married!

He shouts, I do! in his sleep.

Fran perches outside the window, her magpie-sized body blocking the breeze, her eyelids tightly closed. Feathers ripple, the surface of water. Her breasts hang, nipples erect, her body awake.

166

Carmen's eyes stay open so long they sting. She keeps them open on purpose — today is the day Griffin is getting married to someone else. Carmen's jaw tight as tennis racket strings, her tongue dry as salmon jerky. Griffin, that coward. Four A.M., the birds outside chirp and twirp, yodel as if today is no special day.

She has seen Griffin several times but has not attempted to speak to him, call him back, since that day she humiliated herself in front of him in the park while he planted petunias and she was invisible.

She finally meets him in one of the natural food stores, this time by accident. She holds a box of badly needed menstrual tea, he holds a frozen free-range chicken.

Griffin, she says.

167

Hi, he says. Stares at her chin.

Haven't seen you in a while.

Nope.

How's your girlfriend?

Good. Good.

His eyes are dull, Carmen thinks. His skin pink like undercooked red meat.

You wanna go for a cup of coffee? asks Carmen.

Don't think so.

Griffin, she says, touches his coat, breathes in his salty smell. *The Ten Commandments* is playing at the rep theatre this week. D'you want to go see it with me? Remember the last time we saw *The Ten Commandments?* Good old Charlton?

Her hands sweat, her armpits prickle, her chest tightens. Have you ever believed how sorry I am? she asks.

I'm very busy, he says.

Bullshit! she wants to scream. Bullshitting-big-nosed-coward! Her teeth chatter with fury.

Griffin dumps his chicken back in the freezer and walks from the store without looking back.

Carmen goes home and turns on the TV. She's moved the television to the kitchen, and when she's done cooking and eating and washing up the dirty dishes, she'll take the television set with her into the bedroom where she'll set it on the dresser, plug it in and let it sing her to sleep.

She watches another commercial for Aunt Jemima maple syrup and farts in disgust. Aunt Jemima, Uncle Ben, the only black people she sees in the grocery store. Whose Aunt, whose bloody Uncle? She found a tin plaque in an antique store the other day advertising Piccaninny Freeze ice cream. She used to like antique stores back when she was a white girl, now she walks into antique and collectibles stores and all she sees are images of brown people eating watermelons, gobbling fried chicken drumsticks. Tacky representations of Chinese people with pointy hats and bowls of rice. She's been fitted out with some kind of radar over the past year, her skin sensitive to stereotype.

She buys the piccaninny plaque because it stabs her in the heart, she wants to weep at the caricature of a naked little black girl trapped on the sheet of tin, her lips thick and red as the watermelon she holds, huge marble eyes, and her skin charcoal black. Carmen wants to take the little girl home with her, protect her, free her. She pays the clerk and watches as the clerk slides the little watermelon girl into a dark plastic bag.

Don't see much of these things around any more, eh? he says.

Nope.

And she walks the piccaninny out the door by the hand to the safety of her apartment. In the safety of the plastic bag, tucked in a drawer in her bedroom, the piccaninny glows quietly, brighter and more violent than any fire.

She watches black teenagers on the TV arrested and hand-cuffed, their heads forced down. Something about a "Jamaican posse" in central Alberta, says the newscaster.

She collects bits and pieces of information, history, news, images of lynchings and water hoses aimed at people, and stores them in her growing pocket of rage. Sometimes she wraps her hair up in a red bandana like Aunt Jemima. First name "Aunt," surname "Jemima."

Her nostrils flaring, Carmen reads Griffin and Renata's engagement announcement in the paper and marks it down on the calendar with a simple pencilled X. That was six months ago. Tonight she rips the calendar down, tears out the page and burns it over the open toilet where it scorches the porcelain and stinks up the bathroom so bad she thinks the fire alarm might go off, but really she doesn't care.

She has also burned his postcards, letters, and a photo of him she found jammed in the spine of her dictionary.

You know what that's called? says Kevin. That's called pyromania. Pyromania is a severe mental disorder.

Did I ask you over here so you could give me a lecture?

No, you asked me over here because Griffin dumped you.

Dumped me? I dumped him!

That's not what I heard.

So you can't believe everything you hear. How's Sadie?

She's fine.

Oh yeah?

Yeah.

There's no such person as Sadie is there?

Why are you so self-centred?

Because that's why you like me. Keeps you on your toes.

True.

She has seen Griffin driving his truck, sipping coffee out of bowls in the front windows of trendy cafés. She met Griffin's girlfriend, the *fiancée* once, soon after the natural food store brush-off. Renata, sounds like rennet, rhymes with ferret. Griffin and the girlfriend leaving a movie theatre, she and Kevin, walking directly towards them. They are the only people on the sidewalk and the two couples head directly for one another on the narrow sidewalk. Her stomach shrivels to the size of an ancient peanut and her hands shake.

Griffin nods, his nose bigger than ever, bigger than a zeppelin. Hello Carmen, he says. Oh she should be grateful he spoke to her first, spoke to her at all. She should get down on her knees and thank him for the crumb of that Hello Carmen so graciously tossed in her direction. Just like they barely know each other, just like they've never lived together, never shoved their naked genitals into each other's faces. Hello Carmen — bullshit.

Griffin, she nods.

Luckily she looks terrific right at that moment, lipstick freshly applied, hair newly washed, cheeks red from the cold.

This is Renata, Griffin says. Renata, this is Carmen and Kevin.

Nice to meet you, says Kevin.

Her eyes fix on Renata's hair, the bright fine red curls, practically fuzz, in the wind and the snow, and she wants to touch Renata's hair, see if it is as warm as it is bright. Of course she hates Renata, she has no choice, but looking at her hair, maybe after Griffin and Renata's divorce somewhere down the road, they could be friends. Renata's hair, a beacon.

Renata pulls up the hood of her navy blue coat over her head. Carmen's gaze is interrupted and their tenuous connection broken. No, she can never be Renata's friend, she thinks as she looks at Renata's face. Pasty and plain as a slice of mozzarella. So much is obvious from the two of them, Renata and Griffin, standing together, not touching because they don't need to touch, they are so obviously *together*.

Carmen stuffs her hand into Kevin's jacket pocket and they stomp past Griffin and Renata, onward through the snow. Her hand in Kevin's pocket even though he told her expressly no public displays of affection, one of his girl-friend's friends might see.

Griffin's got himself a nice white girl now, eh? she says to Kevin. Nice and white. Not like the old days: *I've always wanted to have a black woman. Black women turn me on,* he used to say. *I like you in black.* That new girl of his is whiter than stale cheese. Whiter than the dandruff in his hair. Whiter than his harpy of a mother was. Whiter than *I* ever was. I always knew he was a coward. Wish I had the guts to say that to his face.

Why don't you? says Kevin. Just a second, whaddaya mean whiter than you ever were? he asks.

Did I say that? she says. I don't remember.

Whorls and bumps on the bedroom ceiling, the open window blows in dank air at 4 A.M., the day of Griffin's wedding. Carmen's mouth twangs shut.

The wedding carries on, of course it does — this is how things go in real life, not like on TV where the bride suddenly changes her mind and jumps out the window in white satin hoop skirts for whatever reason, her cathedral veil around her head like gorgon hair. Griffin leaves early in the morning, Renata dresses in the specially bought underwear; wire supports jab into the bones between her breasts. She even dabs on a bit of mascara — the tube five years old at least — and her eyelashes gum and stick, bits of black float in her eyes, make them redder and puffier than before.

She slides on her dress, combs and fluffs her hair, tucks in the white orchid — she has no idea what part of her head it's supposed to be stuck on — and walks out the apartment, up the sunny, leafy street and through clouds of pollen before she realizes she's left behind her shoes. Her white and pretty Birkenstock sandals.

Her hair moves only slightly in the draft pumped from Fran's wings. Renata's hair is the only evidence, but Renata has a smell Fran *knows*, a heritage Renata keeps like a swallowed jewel, sees reflected in other women on the street who don't give her a second glance, just another white girl. Whiter than dandruff.

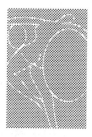

Renata's great-great-grandmother, one slave among many, says Renata's aunt, is left to be eaten by the sun shining through the bars of her cell. She becomes wild ferns, the resting place of flying garbage, broken bottle glass. Animals in the neighbourhood are puzzled by her dead strength, the smell of her sour and exhausted breath. Tourists tip-toe up and down the stone steps, run their fingers along the retaining wall she was forced to hollow out.

Tourists snap each other's pictures, smiles full of the pink of dentures, paper-coloured foreheads perspiring from the heat. Renata's great-great-grandmother appears in the callouses on Renata's hands and the soles of her feet, hard as fingernails, her strong and springy hair, carrot red, a bouquet shouting from the top of her head. Renata sees her own body as veined marble, her great-great-grandmother's blood winding though her and bursting out her scalp.

Schoolgirls in that country, the descendants of slaves, talk about parties and boys while they walk past the old slave monuments, the carefully preserved cages embedded in the stone walls, the cobbled ground. They take shortcuts to school over the ancient blood sucked into the earth. The girls shift from one foot to the other, bored while awed and frightened relatives whisper among the preserved cells, the placid ferns. Their younger brothers and sisters drop bubble gum between the bars of the cells. Giggle about the odour of piss and argue about what's on TV tonight.

Renata smells nothing but the raw meat of Fran's breath, sees only flashes of the blue-black glint of Fran's wings. Fran has kept her obsession with protecting her young one even through death and transformation. Renata feels doubt crawl up and down the front of her dress and into her underpants like fingers.

She returns to the apartment, fits on her Birkenstocks and then walks quickly to make up for lost time. At the courthouse Griffin kisses her on the lips.

You're late, he says. What did you do to your hand?

He doesn't wait for an answer, but presses into her hands a nosegay of orchids and trailing white ribbon to match her hairpiece, and before she knows it she is a married woman, Griffin's wife, Griffin her husband, all in less than an hour.

She holds his hand as they leave the courthouse, she sits in the passenger side of his newly washed, freshly vacuumed truck and they drive to an inner-city park he helped landscape. She gets out of her side of the truck slowly and carefully so that her skirt won't hike up around her hips. She pulls down the hem of the white, lacy mini-skirt with her right hand, holds the creamy nosegay in her left and jumps to the ground. Her toes wink at her from her Birkenstocks. Run away, they say, we dare you. A photographer, hired cheap, stands beside a giant pine tree with a tripod ready and nothing but great wedding photograph ideas.

This weather is perfect, says the photographer. An overcast sky is the best lighting. Testicles! he says and winks, and both Renata and Griffin smile, and he takes their picture.

Renata and Griffin pose in front of pine trees, in beds of daisies, lilies, delphiniums, petunias, standing up, sitting down, together and singly. She leans against a park bench, Griffin's hand in hers, smiling at the camera, he nuzzles his face in her hair under the dragging branches of a weeping willow. Their stomachs begin to grumble with hunger, raindrops begin to fall from the sky. The photographer's already gone through three rolls of film, might as well stop. Head for the apartment so they can freshen up before the party.

Griffin changes his sweaty shirt for a fresh one, combs his hair, brushes his teeth.

Renata drinks a glass of cold water. Sits with her hands stretched out in front of her on the brown wood of the kitchen table. The nosegay rests on the table by her left elbow.

Time to go, missus, yells Griffin, his face wide with the biggest grin in the world; he takes a bite of beef jerky, stuffs it into the breast pocket of his suit jacket. We have to get to the liquor store!

I had an affair, she says.

What?

She picks up the nosegay, tries to undo the bow held securely by wire and glue.

Really he hasn't heard what he thinks he heard, maybe he actually did hear it. He must have heard it, she said it loud and clear like she was telling him it was his turn to do the dishes.

I had an affair.

He takes a breath. He is going to be reasonable, understanding. He is her husband, she is his brand new wife. He will guide her and himself. He doesn't know what's happening, he is about to faint.

Oh yes? When did this happen? he asks.

Yesterday.

Yesterday? Yesterday when?

Yesterday night. When I was late.

Yesterday night. His foot taps the floor of the hallway. Anyone I know?

His mind flashes back to Carmen, stuffing her hand into his now ex-friend Kevin's pocket.

No. I don't think so. No. Definitely not.

So what are you going to do?

I don't know. I don't know what to do.

She looks so much like this is a serious question requiring a serious answer he wants to shake her.

A stretched rubber band in his head breaks.

What do you mean you don't know what to do? We have been married for exactly two hours. You met this person yesterday and now you don't know what to do. You married me two hours ago and you don't know what to do.

No. No I don't. It's not that simple.

We're hardly newlyweds and already you've slept with someone else. This is crazy. This is craziness.

He stalks into the bathroom, lifts up the toilet seat then sets it down.

She wonders why he doesn't just take a piss.

What really bugs me is that you had to bring it up *now*. He kicks his shoes off into the wall. You couldn't keep it to yourself, everyone sleeps around at some point, it's expected, but the *night* before your wedding. The night before our wedding.

She stops picking at the nosegay.

Look, I forgive you for now. Okay. We have a party to get to. We'll pretend everything is the way it should be, we'll talk about this later. We're late. We still have to pick up the case of champagne.

He picks up his shoes and begins to fiddle with the laces, but she can see he's still fuming, toxic fumes ooze from his ears and nose. She coughs and her eyes begin to water.

I can't believe it, he says, shoe in one hand. I can't believe it.

They stand very far apart.

Our wedding day. The day before our wedding. Did those vows mean anything to you? How could you stand there promising to love me forever, to share your life with me forever when you probably still smelled of some other guy's cum?

Now you're being unreasonable! shouts Renata. Her shout erupts from her body and slams into the walls and ceiling, shatters and sprays their bodies.

I'm being unreasonable?

Who are you? she shrieks. I've never met you!

Who are you? he retorts. You're the coldest person I've ever met! I don't want to see you, I don't want to talk to you. Here, he says, and throws the car keys at her. You go to the liquor store!

You don't want me to do that.

He is so angry his voice begins to shake, I've busted my ass for this entire wedding and you have done nothing, absolutely nothing to help except cut up a few fucking carrots. I ask you to go to the liquor store to pick up the champagne you neglected to buy last night no doubt because you were too busy fucking your brains out with some one-night cock-sucker and you don't even want to do that! Frankly, the thought of spending the rest of my life with you makes me want to puke! You will go to the liquor store and pick up the champagne. I will meet you in one hour at the party. End of discussion.

I'll be *happy* to go, she says.

And Renata exits Stage Left forever. She hesitates at the door of the apartment building, but then steps resolutely in the direction of Mika. It's always awkward the morning after.

He won't understand what she's said until much later, a record skipping over and over and over again in his head, especially when he finds out she's having an affair with a woman. Generally, lesbians turn Griffin on, he met some in Europe who were very nice to him, but he doesn't know if he would ever choose to stay involved with one. Renata is the last person he'd expect to be a lesbian, he is not a little shocked when he finds out almost a year after the wedding from a friend of a friend, but he knows he should have guessed when he found out she was incapable of having an orgasm. He thought it was just him, he had lost sleep over her orgasm problem, and now he realizes her protests that no, it wasn't him, it was her, were all fake. Fake fake fake. She just preferred women! She could have told him, he doesn't know why she didn't just tell him at the beginning and save them both a lot of money and anxiety.

After Renata leaves for the champagne, he looks in the mirror and hears the sound of all the money spent by him on this marriage, all of it nonrefundable, and all he wants to do is bite something, bite down hard on a big slab of meat and bone. Instead, he bites the handle of his pink, candy-coloured toothbrush, and his teeth clang down onto the plastic. Lucky his tongue wasn't in the way. The toothbrush remains largely intact, the toothbrush handle marred only by tiny indents.

His suit, rented. Money nonrefundable.

The food and booze, bought and soon to be consumed. Nonrefundable.

Flowers, bought. Nonrefundable.

Tickets to Portugal, bought, nonrefundable because they would have been too expensive otherwise. He can still use at least one of the tickets but he doesn't know where she's keeping them. He scrounges around in her drawers, he wants those tickets, he wants to get out of here away from her as soon as possible, as far away as possible, but she has them hidden somewhere. All he needs is a month, one month away by himself, to get his head together, prepare himself for a life with an adulteress. They'll go through with the reception as planned, then he'll rip up her ticket, take his and leave. See you in a month, baby, he'll say. Make sure you have your shit together by the time I get back, we're in this for life. He pulls all the books from the bookcases, pulls all the chesterfield cushions off onto the floor.

He kicks the bathroom door, the bathroom counter leg, the garbage can so that it skids and sings across the tiled floor and crumpled bits of Kleenex, dental floss, and used sanitary pads wrapped in toilet paper fly from the can as vigorously as freed birds. He holds his hands to his face and they tremble. He rips the lid off the toilet seat and is stunned by his strength.

He is beautiful when he's angry. No one has ever told him this, but his mother Fran, perched on his head, her talons tangled in his hair, sees it.

He dumps Renata's nosegay in the toilet bowl where it floats, an exotic water plant. He presses the flush handle even though he knows the bouquet is too big to go down.

His stomach grinds in on itself, clutches at the leftover bits of food and drops of booze left from his dinner last night. His heart burns, burns from partially digested food rising in his throat, burns from his marriage, failed before it had a chance to begin.

Early the next morning before the sun has risen, he runs still drunk to the park where they had their photos taken. Renata doesn't show up at the party; he tells the guests that she's late, buying extra champagne and snacks, but then she never does show up and he drinks and drinks, may as well humiliate himself completely, first a missing wife and then top it off by getting stinking drunk. The guests embarrassed but they've been drinking for a long time before they figure out the bride isn't going to show. If he'd been sober he would have been embarrassed too, but instead he sits on the prettiest women's laps and smooches in the bathroom with a woman whose name he can't remember but who comforts him with her solid, sweet-smelling body in his arms, her hair like the fur of the hamsters he kept as a child. He and she smack their lips — such delicious, forbidden kisses.

He finds himself on his bed in his apartment still in his clothes at 4 A.M. and still drunk. Renata's luggage, ready for their honeymoon, gone. Good riddance.

In the park Griffin rips open the tool shed, grabs a shovel, then digs and digs and digs. Digs a hole wide enough and deep enough to lie in. The park is dark, silent but for the occasional car driving by just beyond the trees. He sits in his hole, his back and his bum wet from the moist night soil and sweat from all the digging, and he stares at the sky obscured by petunias just above his hole, by tree branches, street lamps and flashing, silent airplanes. Dewdrops dangle in the grass above his head.

He will never speak to Renata again. Never speak to another woman. He will not eat again, sleep again, have sex, ever again. He will run away to a monastery and make cheese and crush grapes with his feet for a living.

Carmen would never have done this to him. Carmen loved him. This thought is enough to send Fran, her only purpose to protect her boy, screaming, a furious homing pigeon.

Of course Griffin will understand when he finds out Renata used the tickets; she couldn't just let them go to waste and besides she paid for them both, he hasn't paid his half yet.

The ticket passes are in a zippered pocket of her carry-on bag, no backpacks this time, and she also carries Mika's passport. Mika almost lost the passport in the airport bathroom, then left it in the waiting area by the gate, she was so flustered and excited.

A month ago, says Mika, if anyone had told me I was going to Europe with the one true love of my life, I would've laughed until my head cracked open. God must be on vacation and forgot to leave a baby-sitter.

Renata and Mika board the plane, Renata's hands eager to clip on her seat belt, fit on her headset, feel the blast of the airplane air conditioning.

Look at the moon, honey! exclaims Mika.

Renata leans sideways across Mika to look out the window. Mika bites Renata's ear, Renata tickles Mika's nipple through the fabric of her t-shirt. Renata lets her head fall back onto her seat cushion. She looks at the back of Mika's head, turned again to the window, strokes Mika's hair, smiles. Mika will love Portugal.

Mika tucks an air-sickness bag into her carry-on bag as a souvenir, she bounces on her seat, stretches her neck to see over the seat in front of her, smooches Renata on the cheek every so often out of simple but overwhelming elation. They are Mrs. Renata Campbell and her travelling companion. Being a married woman will stop people from asking stupid questions, says Mika.

Griffin has faded from sight, the smoke from a pipe. Renata is so tired she can only think of him in pieces, his arm, his belly, the tip of his nose, the smell of his shoulder, and she touches her lover's hand, skin smooth as a newborn chick's.

Carmen stays in bed on Griffin's wedding day. Tells herself she's sick, gradually becomes sick, tastes the tin foil in her mouth that tells her she has a fever. She gets out of bed only to make cups of weak, rapidly cooling tea, then sticks to easy drinks like orange juice. Fran flaps and flaps around the bed, but Carmen isn't sick enough to see her, thinks the odour of Fran's breath is nothing but her own ill farts, Fran's shrieking the spitting of dusty air from the vents.

Carmen's blankets become clammy the longer she sleeps. By the second day, the first day of what she bitterly assumes is Griffin's married life, waves of heat, then cold, travel her body, start at her hips and the small of her back, climb up to her head until she weeps so much she is afraid of drowning. She gets out of bed and crawls around the apartment looking for cooler air, then gets back into bed, shivering. Her body screams with thirst. Orange juice bites into her vocal cords, the walls of her throat.

She trails out of bed, her lips cracked with scum, drapes a wet towel over her head, carries her empty cup to the sink, her head spinning with fever. Over the sink she sees Fran perched on the paper-towel dispenser. Fran with the body of a bird, her skin white as nightmares. Carmen's knees buckle and her head empties. She hasn't spoken out loud for so long her scream is trapped, like flies in spider silk, in the wads of phlegm in her throat.

Her scream creaks and bubbles to a stop, nothing but a stew of sounds. She is able to throw the cup though, throw it hard and throw it mean, so it hits the wall. She swings with her arms, kicks at Fran. She swings, swings and swings, strike one two three, bangs open the fridge door and Fran flies into the fridge in panic, swallowing back the poison she is about to spit in Carmen's face.

Carmen doesn't open the fridge again for three days.

In the fridge, Fran pecks at the thin plastic walls. The shelves on the door filled with watery ketchup, mustard and hardened strawberry jam. She knocks over a can of condensed milk with her right wing, breaks an egg. She scuffles and kicks. Huffs.

She sniffs at an open box of baking soda, breathes on the milk and watches it curdle into white tadpoles. Trapped. She pecks at pieces of tofu, hamburger leftovers. This was not her dream. Now that she can fly, has the free taste for raw meat, the last thing she wants is her wings clipped, her body stuffed into chilly plastic when outside she could be making love with the sky. She thinks of Griffin sprinkling dill seeds among the petunias, and she throws herself against the fridge door. She hears Carmen cough and shuffle, talk miserably on the phone.

Mom, I'm hallucinating. She hears the sound of Carmen crying.

Fran can't stretch her wings or move her body beyond a crouch. She patters around the food, her talons slide through the wires of the shelves. She sits, puffs out her feathers.

I don't know. I don't have a thermometer.

Smell of curdled milk reminds her of little Fran and her pop-eyed nipples, daughter of Bedelia, wife of Godfrey, mother of Griffin, trapped at her shiny, oak dining-room table forcing husband and son to eat her dinner and her words.

Have some more veal, Fran says. Have another sparerib Goddy, Griffin don't gulp your food, chew slowly. Not chewing is unnatural, you're not a coyote in the wild. Chew. Chew. Chew. Chew.

Yeah I'm sick.

Little Fran holding tiny shrivelled Griffin in her arms, does this mean I can't name her Margaret? Fran's arms used to holding school books, flowers. Stupid question, Fran.

I don't know. I don't have a thermometer, I said.

Too young to be having babies, Fran forces Griffin to feed, crams so much food down his throat he throws up, throws up again.

But he's so thin, she tells the doctor. Babies are not supposed to be this thin. She pokes at baby Griffin with her finger, Griffin on the examining table, naked and wriggling.

He's no thicker than a broomstick, she says.

You don't need to exaggerate, get yourself in a panic, says the doctor. Griffin is as natural as babies come. Some babies are just smaller than others.

Fran wanders the house crammed with lights, she is afraid of the dark, husband gone as usual. She wishes she had her mother like other women have — to keep her company, help with the baby and the house. What if she becomes sick? What will happen to Griffin? Her own mother had Vesta for the first few years, why is Fran expected to raise her son on her own?

Griffin grows old enough to go to school and then she is truly alone. Can see the echoes of the television set hit the walls and ricochet straight for her.

The house can only be renovated and re-renovated so many times; she collapses after running in circles from one salmon-coloured wall to the next, stays in bed for days simply because there is nothing else to do. She reads one of God's newspapers while in bed, she circles ads for receptionist work, she can answer phones for heaven's sake. Good Lord you can actually get *paid* to answer a phone! Any dummy can answer phones. She pulls herself out of bed, newspaper in her hand. Wears a scarf over her uncombed hair, pulls on an old dress and checks herself into the nearest beauty salon for the works. Hair, skin, hands, *and* feet.

Do you have today's paper? she asks the receptionist on her way in. Thank you. Is your job particularly difficult? Just answering the phone? Fetching coffee? No, it doesn't look that hard.

What a ridiculously easy job receptionists have. They get paid to answer the phone.

Fran buys a smart suit for her first interview, then her second, her third and fourth. Blouse clean and pressed, hair fluffed and sprayed. Pretty as a poodle in springtime and equally unqualified, but eager for anything, anything.

Six A.M. she wakes up Griffin, scrubs his face, brushes his hair, fixes his breakfast and hurries him off to the neighbours still half asleep.

Then she travels to the building where she works, a red brick building in a semi-respectable neighbourhood, climbs the stairs smelling of Murphy's oil soap and floor cleanser. Her mother would never have allowed her to work *and* be Griffin's mother. She is older than the other girls who work in her office, doesn't make close friends with any of them because they are always leaving, either to get married or have babies. Eight months later when she and Godfrey dine at the restaurant run by Chinese people (she's too tired to cook) she hardly recognizes the New Boss at the other table, sitting alone. He reads something that looks like, probably is, a report.

The New Boss looks so lonely eating his soup — small, thinning hair combed over his pathetic bald spot.

Hey! she calls, and he jumps. I notice you're alone, she says, her eyes large under her poodly cloud of hair. Would you like to join my husband and me for dinner?

She only glances at Godfrey, knowing that he will agree, he will damn well agree.

The New Boss paddles at his soup with his spoon, sips cautiously at his drink, really he should be eating something much thicker, healthier. She just wants to take him to her, feed him and fire him up, see him move with a full-stomached passion. She pats her hair. There can be no strands out of place when she wants to think properly.

The bones in his little bum cut into her thighs he is so thin, but they kiss strongly that first time, the following morning. He sits in her lap, then they kiss a little more gently.

For once she is in control, the larger of the two, cracks him open and carries parts of him away; a pearl of her own, he peers at her through the lenses of his glasses, a naked oyster. He loves her in a way she likes, discreetly, almost entirely clothed.

His first gift to her is a wooden inlay picture of three negroes.

It's beautiful, she says. Where did you get it?

Bermuda, he says.

Bermuda! she says, out of breath. And she puts it away in a downstairs room where it will hardly be noticed, but where she notices it every time she goes to do the laundry, sometimes not even to do laundry but only to *look,* run her fingers over the fine and expensive colours of the wood, ebony for the skin, the real gold leaf of the frame and earrings of the people.

She leaves Griffin with God's mother when the New Boss takes her on her first business trip. Victoria. Land of the newlywed and the nearly dead, Bedelia used to say. For Fran the land of the godless, a green so fresh it's obscene — gigantic blossoms genitalia pink. The New Boss and Fran stroll the Parliament building grounds, the lawns so uniform she wants to jump into them, dog paddle in their luxuriousness.

She allows herself to be vulnerable, lets him kiss her fingers by the fountain, beautiful if she could forget all the urine and spit and God knows what churning and sudsing in the fountain water. She throws in a penny, steps back so none of the water splashes on her, watches the penny glide sideways and sideways to the blue ceramic tiles on the floor of the fountain. She doesn't need to wish for anything. Fresh as a newlywed.

Fran and the New Boss drive through the Crowsnest Pass, their car whizzing through the dust, over the road poured and paved over the rubble of Turtle Mountain. At the gas station the soles of Fran's feet get itchy when she thinks she might be walking over parts of bodies; someone's skull might be looking up through the ground, up under her skirt. She trips over a large rock, a rock the size of a head, and tells the New Boss to take her out of the Pass immediately, she's getting the creeps. The rock watches Fran sadly, rolls away and down a slope.

Wrong place at the right time Miss Regina from Regina crosses the prairies west, talks and kisses her way sweet through the boys and men who work the train tracks for train passage. Walks and hitches wagon rides in her new red kid boots until she stops at the town of Frank for a day and night, invited by a married girlfriend, put up in an airy farmhouse. Tuesday, April 28, 1903.

Town under a mountain round as a turtle's back, never seen a turtle but sure tastes nice in soup she's heard; half-dressed she listens, but no such thing as time that morning 4:10 A.M. April 29, 1903, listens to the turtle's shell slide off and onto the town of Frank, she listens and chills, clasps her hands together, runs to the window to close the sound out, stop the rising of the fine blonde hairs on her arms, the back of her neck. Limestone smashes impolite through her door and windows and walls, smashes in before she can even move from the spot, and she transforms, quick as a car crash, soft sweet flesh and kissy lips harden, her blood stops and clogs, turns to gravel and veins of coal. Miss Regina from Regina grinds to a stop, she is no longer a woman but a woman-shaped bit of mountain holding out her arms to the rocks that come flowing through her door.

When 90 million tons of Turtle Mountain hit where she stands, a human-shaped chunk of stone from Regina, her petrified breasts dislodge and bounce away, chink sparks, her belly shatters into white limestone air, and her pretty, pretty head gallops and sparks across the valley with the mass of skidding mountain to where the highway will be hewn and poured. One boot, new red kid, lies where she used to be, laid out to dry, and bits of her body are carried away in tourist pockets, shut up under museum glass, scattered through the streets, dusted on Fran's black patent leather pumps, the floor of the company car.

Fran listens to the other, younger women at work, their problems, their affairs, their husbands' affairs, and she wonders what the whole to-do is about, it is so easy to split herself down the middle, remain Godfrey's wife and Griffin's mother as well as make room in her lover's appointment book when she wants him. Griffin is too busy doing his own things after all; she watches in salmon-pink, renovated silence as he closes himself off from her, goes out with his friends, sleeps later and later while she works her fingers to the bare bone at the office, then at home.

Fran's mind feeds itself, she learns to feed herself, shows Griffin she loves him by feeding him, insisting he be home for supper, this is the one thing she asks, this is their quality time. Watches him eat dinners mouthful by mouthful. He is still thin as a broomstick but at least now he keeps down his food, until he gets on that vegetarian kick of course, asks for second, third and fourth helpings while she swallows her own dinners down with glasses of white wine or bottled sparkling water, her one treat to herself. She shows her loyalty to God by never running away, resisting the impulse to fly. Keeps clean and orderly their nest, keeps his son in order as best she can. Trapped in her fine and expensive house, a bird in a cage.

For Fran, a life of secrets is the only life to have. She realizes this in the cut-glass vases full of dried flowers in winter, fresh flowers in summer, vases she could never afford on her own meagre salary. She needs God and she needs her job. She also needs Griffin. They give her permission.

Fran's in my fridge, his mother's in my fridge! You're supposed to be dead, shrieks Carmen, you're supposed to be fucking dead! I'm not letting you out until you're deader than a fucking doorknob! Doornail! No, doorknob!

Fran begins to weep, her eyes without whites, same colour as her nipples, leak, then pour. God is forgiving when he finds out, forgiveness is part of his nature, maybe it was the New Boss's smell on her that gave her away though she always bathed so thoroughly. God responds only by packing down the tobacco in his pipe so hard the bowl of the pipe breaks off and tobacco scatters all over the carpet. She says nothing about the mess.

Do you love him? asks God. Specifically, do you love him more than you love me?

Of course not, she says. Tears dripping down both sides of her mouth flow freely from her nose, she doesn't even allow herself a Kleenex, unfaithful that she is, but lets the tears drip and drip, wipes them only with the sleeves of her favourite silk blouse. Now ruined. She doesn't deserve him.

God stays home then, stays home for seven months, longer than he's ever stayed home since the first days of their marriage. They do appropriate things together, always together and she is never out of his sight or beyond his smell, he picks her up and drops her off at work. Eats lunch with her, sleeps with her. He prowls and haunts the house, smokes and smokes until the downstairs floor of the house is dense with haze, but he never speaks. His silence, his forgiveness, is a boulder crushing the muscles in her neck, snapping her vertebrae. Her stomach and innards seize with guilt so strong even laxatives can't free her. She takes to winding rubber bands around her wrists, the digits of her fingers, once even around her neck. But she desires life. She wishes he would scream and storm — God's forgiveness is the worst.

God asks to see the New Boss.

Pardon me?

I want to meet him officially. I want to talk to him. You're my wife. I want to make that as clear to him as possible.

And she wants to shake him, just shake him by his immense shoulders and long glorious hair, tell him, No, this job is mine! My life is mine! Go away and stay away!

All right, she says and suddenly her power over the New Boss is as elusive as a penny sinking in a fountain.

The two men shake hands and grumble, she sits between them on a stool, pretty and useless, not that she expects a fight but they may require a mediator. They all three eat their lunch, though she barely touches hers, her stomach too upset anyway, but God gets drunker and drunker, drinks beer after beer after beer. She wishes he would drink something a little more classy, since it is the middle of the day. He rams the leg of his chair through the plasterboard wall of the restaurant when he gets up to go for a piss. So far he has said nothing.

Oh I'm so sorry, says Fran to the waiter, so sorry, my husband isn't well you see and I'm so sorry. Can I call you and we can settle this or no, here's my phone number, I can send you a cheque once you figure out what the cost for the wall is I'm really very sorry, really I am. So sorry.

She tries not to see the expressions on the faces of the other diners in the restaurant, her face red and her eyes swollen with the backward pain of tears.

She drives Godfrey's car home and he clutches her knee, once her elbow while she's trying to shift the gears.

God yells at the New Boss, So my wife is sure some sweet lay, eh? Guess I don't have to tell you, you know all about how sweet and pretty she is don't you? She good for you? She do what she says she's gonna do? Or does she just lie there like a goddamn hunk of wood, I seen logs got more spunk. You little pencil-necked piece of toad shit. No, I've examined toad shit that's got more guts than you, I study shit for a living and no shit I've ever looked at has been as pencil-necked and pathetic as you. You probably shit pencils your ass is so tight, that's right, shit pencils!

Spit flies from his mouth and sprinkles the inside of the windshield as he laughs at his own joke.

The New Boss sits in the back seat, There now big fella, Hey there big guy, now there's no call for that, he says over and over again, doesn't look at Fran once and pushes his glasses farther onto his nose. She wonders in a crazy moment if this will affect her annual twenty-cent raise, then she moves her hand quickly to where Godfrey has started manipulating the gear shift.

Sweat dapples the New Boss's temples, both men stink of sour perspiration and alcohol. God yells dirty jokes out the window and Fran spins the car down alleyways, gravel spitting up from the road behind.

Griffin is watching television in the front room but then stands still and straight as she and the New Boss help God into the house and into bed where he roars for another beer.

Time to eat, she says to Griffin.

See you on Monday? she says to the New Boss.

Monday, he says, jumps in a cab not looking back.

She pulls cold casserole from the fridge, slices it into squares and puts it under tin foil into the oven.

Why aren't you drinking your milk? Why aren't you eating? Why are you crying? Stop that stop that I thought I said? What do you have to cry about?

I'm crying for myself, says Griffin.

Fran takes another sip of wine. You go on and watch TV then, she says. She stabs a fork into her thigh, hard enough to draw blood and shred her stocking, then continues picking at her casserole.

Fran, calls God from the bedroom. I don't care what you do. As long as you don't ever love anyone more than you love me.

Fran's tear ducts ooze nothing but single grains of sand.

Carmen's mother opens the fridge, and Fran slides out invisible, her tears and woman-self left on the food in clumps of soft mould. Fran's breasts and face now shrunk and covered with feathers, her mouth long and sharp the way a magpie's should be.

Transformation complete.

The New Boss digs his fingers into the top of his head and hollows out a cave between the shifting and sliding plates of his skull. He jumps onto his desk; his feet make scuff marks and crumple his papers, the heel of his shoe crushes the window of a calculator and he crouches, melts, hollows and hollows out his skull until he is nothing but a holder for pencils. God knows he has no purpose now that Fran is truly gone.

Fran flies, flaps her wings harder and her small bird's heart beats quickly. Fran flies high above the city, her wings stretched to their fullest, her beak wide open. God lights a pipe. Griffin sprinkles thyme seeds in the kale. The New Boss holds ten new pencils and three paper clips.

Fran breathes in the soft, polluted air, extends her skinny, feathered arms as far as they can go, sees nothing but the sun.

When Carmen surfaces from her flu, she looks around the apartment which her mother has scrubbed so clean the walls try to hide. Carmen gets out of bed and carries the television to the bathroom. She uses an extension cord to plug the TV into an outlet in the hallway.

She opens the fridge; Fran is gone. Carmen's mother told her that Fran left, so Carmen can open the fridge whenever she wants to. The fridge, nicely defrosted and still smelling faintly of detergent. Carmen pulls out a Tupperware container packed with pieces of cold fried chicken left by her mother.

She prepares a bubble bath. The feel of clean, hot water splashing over her fingers gives her goose pimples. She brushes her teeth, scrubs with the bristles at the anger coating her tongue, dislodges her hate from between her teeth with dental floss. Carmen slides into the water and

210

watches the television screen. Her hair is tied up in an Aunt Jemima red bandana. She is a single girl living in a one-bedroom apartment; she would like to be married, her biological clock has started ticking so loudly she can't sleep at night, but she supposes she will have to wait. She will settle for being single and sleeping alone for the time being. Besides, she's not ready to go through the hell of looking for another wedding dress. A single girl slicing her teeth through the salty, lovely, greasy skin of a nice fried leg of chicken — she has always loved fried chicken. Always. Even in the old days. She wasn't so bad in the old days, just a little naive. Maybe she should get a roommate, television is boring. Or a satellite dish, that might be even better.

She has always loved TV. Always. Even in the pink days. A roommate could never compare to a good sit-com or a slick documentary.

Being a brown girl almost feels like being drunk. She tries to remember the days when she was white and sober, but she can only think of herself as brown— as having always been brown, so that she marvels at how well she pulled off being white. Fooled them all, fooled everyone, even herself, the best magic trick of all. A reverse Oreo cookie, an inside-out coconut, the juice running down the sides and spilling all over the floor. Now she is brown and drunk out of her mind. She's sipped and gulped so much she's drunk, drunk out of her skull, dead drunk, past drunk, so drunk she's sober, her mind as sharp and bright as the point of a new needle. That's what being a white girl turned brown girl is all about. Or a brown girl who was brown all along but nobody knew, not even herself. Only now learning to enjoy the taste of the drink, not just an intoxicating cocktail, but an empowering elixir.

Carmen wipes her nose with the sudsy washcloth, contemplates her heart floating in many pieces on the water covering her body. She would like to say she is no longer in love. She would like to say that her flu stripped her and cleansed her, that now she is ready to leave the safety of her TV. She would like to think that she no longer needs the comfortingly greasy and magic feel of dark lipstick on her lips, pitch black mascara on her eyelids, or her cocoon of an apartment. She would like to think that she will never again try to run into Griffin, have sex with him in her mind, or imagine the gorgeous genius children they might have had together. She would like to believe that now she has all the answers, can defrost her own refrigerator, will finally get her shit together enough to go out and buy her own thermometer.

Wrong.

She picks up the phone, punches in Griffin's number. She will be friendly and nonthreatening. Just wanted to wish you a happy marriage, she'll say, she's a good sport. We can be friends, she'll say, her mind sharp, shockingly brilliant. If the wife answers, Carmen will hang up the phone.

The world is a tidy place.

References

Bride's magazine. *Bride's All New Book of Etiquette.* New York, N.Y.: Putnam Publishing Group, 1993.

Ovid. *Metamorphoses.* Translated by Mary Innes. Middlesex, U.K.: Penguin Books, 1955.